SHADOW
SQUADRON

ELITE
INFANTRY

WRITTEN BY
CARL BOWEN

ILLUSTRATED BY
WILSON TORTOSA

COLORED BY

YOUNG READERS

INTEL

2019.681

Shadow Squadron is published by
Capstone Young Readers,
A Capstone Imprint,
1710 Roe Crest Drive
North Mankato, MN 56003
www.capstoneyoungreaders.com

Cataloging-in-Publication Data is
available on the Library of Congress
website.

ISBN: 978-1-62370-032-4 (paperback)

Summary: Lieutenant Commander Cross is
given a job offer he can't refuse: command
an elite squad of soldiers tasked with
tackling military ops that are blacker than
black and far beyond the call of duty.

Designed by Brann Garvey
Edited by Sean Tulien

Printed in China by Nordica.
0413/CA21300521
032013   007226NORDF13

CONTENTS

MISSION ONE
SEA DEMON 7

MISSION TWO
BLACK ANCHOR 63

MISSION THREE
EAGLE DOWN 117

MISSION FOUR
SNIPER SHIELD 171

1316.981

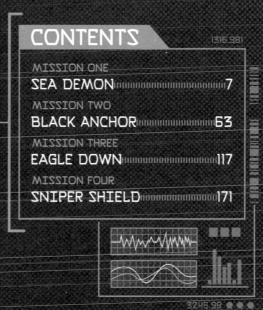

3248.98 ● ● ●

2012.101

CLASSIFIED

SHADOW SQUADRON

CROSS, RYAN

RANK: Lieutenant Commander
BRANCH: Navy SEAL
PSYCH PROFILE: Cross is the team leader of Shadow Squadron. Control oriented and loyal, Cross insisted on hand-picking each member of his squad.

WALKER, ALONSO

RANK: Chief Petty Officer
BRANCH: Navy SEAL
PSYCH PROFILE: Walker is Shadow Squadron's second-in-command. His combat experience, skepticism, and distrustful nature make him a good counter-balance to Cross's leadership.

YAMASHITA, KIMIYO

RANK: Lieutenant
BRANCH: Army Ranger
PSYCH PROFILE: The team's sniper is an expert marksman and a true stoic. It seems his emotions are as steady as his trigger finger.

BRIGHTON, EDGAR

RANK: Staff Sergeant
BRANCH: Air Force Combat Controller
PSYCH PROFILE: The team's technician and close-quarters-combat specialist is popular with his squadmates but often agitates his commanding officers.

LARSSEN, NEIL

PHOTO NOT AVAILABLE

RANK: Second Lieutenant
BRANCH: Army Ranger
PSYCH PROFILE: Neil prides himself on being a jack-of-all-trades. His versatility allows him to fill several roles for Shadow Squadron.

SHEPHERD, MARK

PHOTO NOT AVAILABLE

RANK: Lieutenant
BRANCH: Army (Green Beret)
PSYCH PROFILE: The heavy-weapons expert of the group, Shepherd's love of combat borders on unhealthy.

LOADING MISSION:

SEA DEMON

CLASSIFIED

MISSION BRIEFING

SEA DEMON 1234

Well-organized Somali pirates have kidnapped several civilians at sea, including a V.I.P. from the World Food Program. The abductions occurred in international waters, meaning that any miscues on our part will reflect negatively on the United States at large. We have been tapped to put these pirates down before innocent blood is shed. Even though we operate in the shadows, all eyes are on us for this one, gentlemen.

— Lieutenant Commander Ryan Cross

SOMALIA

PRIMARY OBJECTIVE

- Secure hostages and transport them to safety

SECONDARY OBJECTIVES

- Neutralize all enemy combatants while minimizing loss of life

- Identify possible leads in preventing future attacks by pirates

1932.789

0412.981

1624.054

SEA DEMON

Lieutenant Commander Ryan Cross stood up to check his parachute rigging one more time. As he did, a scrawny aerospace physiology tech prodded Cross in the shoulder. Cross let the tech examine him without saying anything. Standing room was limited in the rear of the brand-new MC-130J Commando II aircraft, but Cross appreciated the tech's presence. The plane was well over 25,000 feet high in the starlit black sky. No matter how fit and healthy a soldier was, the pressure and cold at that altitude could play havoc on his body. It was the tech's job to make sure that didn't happen.

Cross and his men had been breathing pure oxygen for a while now. It was the only way to keep deadly nitrogen bubbles from forming and expanding in their blood at that altitude. But with the two-minute jump warning approaching, the physiology tech was giving the jump team a last checkup. He examined them for signs of hypoxia, narcosis, or other pressure-related ailments. A single problem could take one of the men out of action before Operation Sea Demon was even underway.

The two-minute warning sounded. Cross endured the tech's last-minute tests while also double-checking the rigging of the soldier in front of him. Muscle memory from dozens of previous jumps made his hand want to clip a ripcord carabiner to a static line at shoulder height. However, this wasn't going to be a static-line jump. It was to be a high-altitude, high-opening or HAHO free-fall. Other than in training exercises with his former SEAL unit, Cross had never attempted a nighttime HAHO jump.

The tech leaned in close to Cross so he could be heard over the howl of wind and engine noise from the open rear hatch. "Your pulse is elevated," the tech said.

Cross's only answer was a Cheshire-Cat grin.

The tech rolled his eyes in an exaggerated manner. "All right, Commander," he said. "You and your men are all clear to jump."

"Good to go, gentlemen!" Cross called over the tech's shoulder.

"HOORAH!" Shadow Squadron replied in unison.

Cross set down his oxygen mask. With one last glance at his watch, he signaled his men to move toward the rear of the plane where the jumpmaster waited.

As one, the men switched to bottled oxygen. They flipped down the night-vision scopes mounted on their helmets. Then

they filed out the back as the jumpmaster gave them the go-ahead.

One after another, in perfect form, the members of Shadow Squadron dropped from the dimly red-lit interior of the MC-130J into the starlit darkness.

Cross was the last man out. He hurled himself into the void without fear or hesitation. Like a true soldier.

It was only a matter of seconds before the first man out the hatch, Staff Sergeant Edgar Brighton, flattened out of his power dive. He spread-eagled in the air to maximize wind-resistance. The other skydivers above him immediately did the same. They all spread out into their assigned positions and simultaneously opened their chutes. The jolt of deceleration nearly knocked the wind out of Cross — and very nearly tore the mouthpiece of his oxygen bottle from his mouth. Cross pushed through the pain and wheeled around to link up with his team.

With quick precision, the soldiers glided into position one above the other. Still thousands of feet up in the air, they settled into a vertical stack for the long, long trip down.

Far below the soldiers lay a vast, featureless ocean. The team was headed to a tiny uncharted jungle island in the Indian Ocean east of the Horn of Africa. At the bottom of the stack, Brighton was responsible for directing the team.

Cross had full faith in Brighton's capabilities. Sergeant Brighton was a well-trained and highly competent US Air Force combat controller. Despite being the youngest man on the team, Brighton had more nighttime jumps under his belt than all of his squadmates combined. Brighton would get them where they needed to go. Cross had no worries about that. All Cross could do now was settle in for the long glide and prepare himself for the mission ahead.

As he fell through the endless dark, Cross couldn't help but reflect back on the sequence of unbelievable events that had led him to this night.

* * *

A year ago, Ryan Cross had been a "mere" Navy SEAL. He'd served tours in Afghanistan and Iraq. He'd worked behind enemy lines in the deserts, mountains, and half-ruined cities of those nations. His teams had greatly assisted the efforts of the military in the War on Terror. Through raging fire, blinding sand, and shed blood, his actions had been crucial to the war's success.

Cross's team brought down terrorist networks and undermined criminals who were thriving in the ongoing chaos of warfare. Cross had never wanted awards or acclaim for his efforts. But when his last tour had ended, he knew he'd made his country — and fellow soldiers — proud.

Cross had thought that would be the end of it. With his duty done, he figured he'd return home to find a regular job, marry a nice girl, and maybe have some kids.

However, the US government had other plans for him. Just minutes before he was scheduled to board the plane that would take him home, a young corporal approached him.

"Sir!" the corporal said. He popped off a quick salute. "I need you to come with me, Commander. It's urgent, sir."

"I see," Cross said. He couldn't help glancing at the plane waiting to take him home as it idled on the tarmac.

"I'll tell them to hold your seat," his lieutenant said. Cross nodded and handed off his duffel bag to one of the airplane workers.

Cross followed the corporal over to the Humvee. He ducked into the cool interior of the vehicle. Waiting in the back was an unexpected — and unwelcome — face. It belonged to Bradley Upton, a CIA operative who had worked with Cross in the past.

"Ryan," the spook said as Cross sat down.

"That's Lieutenant Commander Cross," he said coolly.

"Still?" Upton said with a smirk.

The young corporal hopped in behind Cross. He slammed the door shut and the driver peeled out. The rumble of the engine was so loud that Cross could barely hear himself think, much less ask Upton what the situation was.

Thirty minutes later, the Humvee wheeled into the Victory Base Complex near Baghdad. The base served as the nerve center for US operations in Iraq. The corporal hurried Cross out of the Humvee and led him into the main building, followed by Upton. The corporal threaded them through a bustling crowd of soldiers of countless ranks and job descriptions toward an unmarked office. When Cross and

Upton entered, the corporal remained outside and shut the door behind them.

An impressive oak desk was at the center of the otherwise nearly empty room. When Cross realized who was sitting at the desk, his jaw dropped. Cross had never met the man personally, but anyone who'd watched CNN since the war started would recognize him.

Cross snapped to attention and saluted like a new recruit. "General," he said. "I didn't realize you were back in the country already, sir."

The general waved off the salute. "No need to be so formal, Commander," he said. He gestured to the two seats across the desk from him. Upton had already taken one of them. "Have a seat."

The general produced a folder from a drawer in his desk. He recited the highlights of Cross's service record as he read from the file. The general maintained a neutral expression as he read off the list of Cross's many accomplishments and numerous awards.

After several minutes of recitation, the general stopped. "I'm impressed, Commander," he said. "Which is why you're here. I know your hitch is just about over, and I'm told you haven't signed up for another tour. I want you to reconsider."

Cross tried unsuccessfully to hide his confusion. "Sir?" he asked. The general wasn't even in the Navy like Cross was. Why would he care whether Cross applied for more active duty?

"I'm not talking about the Navy," the general said, understanding Cross's confusion. "No, I've got something different in mind for you. Joint Special Operations Command has selected you to head a special missions unit. It would be an entirely new, secret program. You're not obligated to accept. But if you don't, I can't tell you any more than I already have."

Cross felt his eyebrows rise in curiosity. The special missions units of the US Special Operations Command were the elite of the elite in the armed forces. It was an honor to even be considered for such a position.

"If I may ask, sir," Cross began. He nodded toward Upton without looking at him. "What's he doing here?"

"We here at the Joint Special Operations Command have a history of respectful cooperation with the CIA," the general said. "Agent Upton here performs field evaluations of soldiers who we're considering to join us."

Upton showed a slick smile. "Yours was a particular pleasure," he said. "Remember Baqubah? You impressed a lot of people that day. Even me."

Before Cross could say anything, the general said, "In return for his occasional service, we give Agent Upton opportunities like this one to try to steal candidates from us. The CIA has a paramilitary Special Operations Group of its own. Upton wants you to lead it."

"It's harder work, and it's more dangerous," Upton said. "But the pay's better. A lot better. Our operators have more freedom in the field, too. You've seen *Mission: Impossible*, I'm sure? Well, that's kindergarten compared to what we do." Upton sat back with a satisfied look on his face.

"So that's why you're here, Lieutenant Commander," the general said. "You've got a choice to make between us and the CIA. Or you can just walk out the door and get on that plane with the thanks of a grateful nation for the service you've already given."

"Which, in today's economy and job market," Agent Upton said, "would be pretty stupid, if you ask me."

Cross stared at the folder on the general's desk. Slowly, he thought through the surprising choice set before him. Without raising his eyes, he said, "One thing I've never been is stupid."

Upton clapped Cross on the shoulder. He rose with a triumphant expression on his face. "Smart choice," he said. "Then let's get —"

"I'm in, General," Cross said, lifting his eyes at last. He reached across the desk and shook hands with the older man.

"Excellent," the general said. "Welcome to Shadow Squadron."

* * *

The long year that followed was filled with training and more training. Shadow Squadron was comprised of elite soldiers from every branch of the military. The goal was to have the group function independently anywhere in the world. As such, every operator had to be trained in relevant skills that his native military branch hadn't taught him.

For the first couple of months, Cross met and accepted command of his new team and organized a training schedule for his men. For the rest of the year, the unit lived, drilled, and trained together. They learned to build on each other's strengths. From a group of very different soldiers, Cross forged a cohesive unit that operated as one. All that remained after the endless training was to get the team into the field and prove it could handle a real mission.

That opportunity finally came one week ago. The trouble started in the Arabian Sea.

For years, the shipping lanes that pass through the Indian Ocean, across the Arabian Sea, and through the Gulf of Aden had been a treacherous feeding ground for Somali pirates. At first, the pirates were simply frustrated Somali fishermen doing whatever they could to protect their coastal fishing waters from other countries' commercial fishing ships. With the Somali navy in shambles after the country's civil war, there was no one else who could help.

As their early efforts proved successful, many of the desperate fishermen evolved into professional criminals. Their operations grew in size and complexity. Soon, their piracy began to extend farther and farther from the Somali shore. They began ransoming hostages and stealing cargo for profit. Some of these pirates had grown as rich and powerful as any warlord on land.

Every nation that had been affected by these criminals took steps to fight the pirate menace. They dispatched warships to the area. They trained their merchant ship crews to defend themselves. These measures were effective and drove down piracy rates significantly.

There were also many notable military successes against pirate operations. The US Navy SEALs liberated the captured *Maersk Alabama*, which increased confidence that the waterways were getting safer. Yet, for every *Maersk Alabama* incident with a happy ending, there were dozens more that went unreported or ended in the outlaws' favor.

The pirates weren't going away any time soon. The incident that called Cross's Shadow Squadron into action was proof of that.

In the dead of one summer night, a World Food Program cargo vessel loaded with food aid and medical supplies had been attacked and boarded. In international waters, a pair of pirate motorboats launched from a mother ship, circling the WFP ship like sharks. Using AK-47s, the pirates easily subdued the crew and the vessel. Then, as far as anyone could tell, the pirates and their stolen vessel disappeared.

Before any ransom demands could be delivered, a distress call went out from the captured ship via satellite phone. Hiding aboard the cargo vessel, the caller was able to make contact with the US Navy a few times. But the pirates quickly found him and silenced him.

A satellite trace gave Naval Intelligence enough intel to guess where the pirates might have been headed. However, no ships on patrol had been able to find the pirates. A day

later, new satellite recon discovered the pirates' hideout —
a tiny uncharted jungle island — just as they were towing the
captured vessel to shore.

That day, anonymous ransom demands went out. They
wanted $20 million for every hostage — except one. For the
last hostage, they wanted $50 million. It was likely the last one
had been the man they'd caught calling for help. The pirates set
a one-week deadline.

As Cross relayed this information to his squad, he saw
Chief Petty Officer Alonso Walker narrow his eyes. Cross
knew that Walker was about to interrupt his briefing.

Walker had come out of the SEAL teams like Cross, but
he'd been in service several years longer. As Cross's second-in-
command, Walker seemed to resent Cross's perceived lack of
special operations experience.

"Who is he?" Walker asked. "Who made the calls?"

"His name's Alan Smithee," Cross explained. "He's the
documentary filmmaker who shook up the presidential
primaries last year. His new film is about the alleged corruption
in the World Food Program."

"Looks like he got a little more trouble than he bargained
for," Walker said. "Do we know who has him?"

"I was getting to that," Cross said flatly. "Based on the
information he was able to give us, we believe the pirates who
attacked the ship belong to the Shayatin al-Bahar group. They
operate out of the port city of Kismayo in southern Somalia.

They claim to be supported by the Islamic Courts Union. But CIA analysts have proven that their money and weapons are provided by al-Qaeda."

Cross knew that two of his men had been born and raised in New York. So he paused briefly to observe their reactions at the mention of the terrorist group. Jaws were clenched and muscles were stiff, but there were no emotional outbursts. That was good. His men needed to remain calm, even when things hit close to home.

"We almost scooped up the leader, whom we only know as 'Malik al-Bahar,'" Cross continued, "in a raid on the group's base of operations in 2005. Somebody tipped them off, though, and the leaders vanished. From what little intel we have on this Malik fella, we know he's built his operation back up. Lately, he's been launching attacks in the Indian Ocean and Arabian Sea. He launders ransom money through intermediaries, so we've never been able to track him. Efforts to uncover his supply chain haven't turned up anything, either."

"So what we've got here, men," Walker said, cutting in, "is a rare opportunity to raid this pirate gang's new base of operations. And then tear it down once and for all." He stood to face the men beside Cross as if he were suddenly the one running the briefing.

"Thank you, Chief," Cross said tightly. "But our first priority is to rescue those hostages. We know where they're going to be, and the pirates don't know we know. All other objectives are secondary to that."

Walker frowned. "If those are your orders —"

"They are," Cross said. "Now take a seat. We have a lot to get through."

* * *

Walker had interrupted several more times during the briefing. He seemed more tense and agitated with each interjection. He obviously resented Cross's leadership.

But now, as they glided through the night sky, Cross saw that Walker was dialed in and focused on the landing point, which was a good thing. The landing point was an island whose sole inhabitants were vicious seaborne killers. They had no respect for international law. They viewed human lives as mere bargaining chips. They had earned the moniker "Sea Demons" in every way.

Cross saw that the landing point was drawing near. He sucked a deep, cleansing breath from his oxygen bottle to clear his mind. It was time to get to work.

Cross's team left their vertical stack a few hundred yards out from the coast of the pirates' hidden island. For the rest of the descent, they drifted downward as close together as they could safely manage.

Touching down, most squad members landed on the beach. But Lieutenant Kimiyo Yamashita — an Army Ranger, and the team's sniper — caught a cross-wind. He came up short, splashing down in the dark water. Sergeant Brighton didn't touch ground until he passed through the tree line ahead. Initiating noise discipline, Cross signaled the men to gather up their chutes and head into the jungle after Brighton. Cross waited for Yamashita to wriggle out of his jump rigging and swim to shore. Then the two of them followed the others.

Under cover of trees, the men began burying their jump gear. When Brighton finished burying, he lifted his special-issue panoramic night-vision goggles and looked over at Cross. With a grin on his face, Brighton pointed at himself with both thumbs and tilted his head, as if asking: How'd I do? Cross gave him a thumbs-up. Brighton grinned even wider.

Cross then moved toward Chief Walker and signaled that he wanted eyes on the perimeter. Walker nodded curtly and chose three men, a Ranger and two Green Berets, to scan for trouble while the rest of the team set up. The scouts tapped two-way earphones nestled in their right ears to test the signal, then headed into the jungle.

Meanwhile, Yamashita shrugged off his heavy backpack. Brighton helped set it on the ground and carefully wiped the excess moisture off the waterproof case. Then he pulled out a metal suitcase and a tablet computer from the pack. Inside the metal case was a two-stick remote control and a black reconnaissance unmanned aerial vehicle, or UAV. It was about the size of a Roomba robot vacuum cleaner. This UAV was one of a kind, designed and built by Brighton himself. He gently lifted it out of the case as if it were his newborn son.

With a nod from Cross, Brighton turned on the tablet computer and synced it up with the UAV and the controller.

With a faint click, Brighton thumbed on the UAV's engine. Its four internal whisper-quiet propellers came to life and lifted the UAV to eye level, where it hovered steadily. Like a kid with a new toy, Brighton sat cross-legged beneath the UAV with the tablet on his lap. He switched back and forth on the screen for the front and rear views, checking the feeds from the UAV's cameras. The clarity was perfect.

Brighton raised and lowered the UAV a few feet. Then he made it spin in place one way, then the other. Lastly, he made the UAV glide around the other four soldiers. The device barely made a sound as it hovered a few feet above their heads.

The young combat controller was testing the equipment, but Cross figured Brighton was also showing off a little. So when Brighton looked up at Cross with a grin on his face, Cross held up his wrist and tapped his watch. Brighton got the message.

His grin gone, Brighton sent the UAV up through the trees and out of sight. Carefully, he scanned the area from above. The lookouts hadn't called in any warnings yet, which led Cross to believe the pirates had no idea his men had arrived. Cross relaxed noise discipline, but radioed his lookouts to stay where they were for the moment.

"Any sign of a radar or sonar setup, Brighton?" Chief Walker asked over his shoulder.

"Not that I can tell, Chief," Brighton said. His voice was hushed and respectful. "Nothing on this end of the island, anyway."

Walker glanced up at Cross. "So we could have come in by boat or submersible," he said. It wasn't exactly a question. Walker had argued long and hard in the planning phase for a water insertion rather than a HAHO jump.

Brighton noticed the tension between Walker and Cross. "When we get closer, I can take a better look," he said. "They might have something set up on the far side that I can't make out from here."

"That won't be necessary," Walker said. "We're already here. I was just curious."

Cross made no reply to that. He turned to Brighton. "Bring the UAV back, recharge it, and hide it," he said. "Let's go get our eyes on the compound."

"Sir," Brighton said with a nod.

"Call the lookouts back in," Cross said to Walker.

The chief stepped away. With a hand to his ear, he sent the order out via earphone.

* * *

Half an hour later, Cross had moved his team east across the island and closer to the headquarters of the Shayatin al-Bahar. Between binoculars, Brighton's UAV cameras, and Yamashita's sniper scope, the team had a good idea of the hideout's exterior layout. The compound lay within a cliff wall overlooking the northeastern edge of the island. At the top were two concrete structures. One was the pirates' barracks and mess area. The second was an older single-story longhouse with a wooden watchtower. There was a big halogen spotlight at the top.

The light wasn't on at the moment, but there was enough room on the tower platform to move and aim it. In the center of the compound lay a concrete slab with a heavy metal hatch in the center. The hatch led into the interior of the cliff, which connected somewhere with a path to the cave that opened out at the shore. A long footpath on a shallow grade led down to the water's edge from the compound as well.

Brighton's UAV found the pirates' mother ship docked just inside the shelter of the cave. The World Food Program vessel had likely been unloaded and shipped off elsewhere for sale on the black market.

"Anybody have eyes on the hostages?" Walker asked, barely whispering. He, Yamashita, and Second Lieutenant Neil Larssen all lay prone. They were on the edge of a ridge that overlooked the compound about a half-mile away.

Yamashita silently scanned the area through the Leupold scope on his M110 sniper rifle. A moment later, he only shook his head. Larssen lowered his binoculars. He said, "I can see shadows moving inside the longhouse. It's locked and guarded. That has to be where the hostages are."

"Probably," Chief Walker agreed.

Yamashita simply shrugged. He kept scanning the area through his scope. The pirates had bright lights mounted on the longhouse, mess, and barracks. The sniper's scope didn't even need its night sights.

Walker slithered away from the ridge. He knelt next to Brighton, who was packing away the UAV. Next to Brighton, Cross swiped through some of the images the UAV had collected on the tablet. "No positive ID on the hostages," Walker said. "But we think we know where they are."

"Longhouse?" Cross asked without lifting his eyes from the tablet screen.

"More than likely," Walker said.

Cross nodded and softly snapped his fingers to get his men's attention. "Gather 'round," he said quietly. He laid the tablet on the ground before him. All of the men except Yamashita formed up in a tight circle around the tablet computer. It showed a satellite photo of the island, which Cross pinched and zoomed in on to show the operational area that lay below their current location. He tapped the edge of the image, laying down a red dot. "Okay, we are here. The ridge line's here." He traced it. "We've counted thirteen hostiles so far. Seven of our 'Sea Demons' are here, in the mess hall."

Cross tapped another section of the map image, which brought up a short video the UAV had taken of the mess and barracks buildings. The buildings had no guards, but the doors and windows were all open. "One sentry with a spotlight, an AK-47, and an RPG, is here," he said, tapping the appropriate place on the map to mark it. They all watched the UAV's fly-by footage of the sentry. He looked bored, but was wide awake and had his Russian-made automatic rifle slung at the ready near his shoulder. The rocket-propelled grenade launcher stood on end in the corner of the tower platform.

"Two guards with AKs are on the longhouse door," Cross tapped another section of the map to show Brighton's high-angle footage. When the map reappeared, he circled part of the cleared area between the team's hiding spot and the pirate compound. When he tapped that area, footage appeared of a pair of men walking side by side around the compound. "Two mobile sentries on the perimeter. Armed with AKs. Probably radios. Guard on the tower has one, too."

Cross brought up more footage. "No guards on the path down the long way around the cliff, but they've got at least one man on the boat," Cross said. "No sign of how extensive the cave system is beyond their hidden harbor, but there could be at least one stairway up from below." Cross stood up and tapped his earphone. "Is there any activity on that hatch, Yamashita?"

"Nobody's gone in or out," came Yamashita's quiet reply through the team's earpieces.

"Then here's the plan," Cross said. "Yamashita, stay where you are for overwatch. Paxton, you'll spot for him."

"Sir," both men said.

"Williams, you're coming with me," Cross ordered. "We'll get into the longhouse and check the status of the hostages."

"Sir," the team's corpsman said.

"Walker, you'll take Brighton, Shepherd, and Larssen with you," Cross said. "I want you to flush the seven off-duty pirates into the mess and subdue them."

"Should we try to take them prisoner?" Walker asked.

Cross's face took on a grim look. "It's not a priority," he said. Part of him hoped the pirates would simply drop their weapons when they saw armed men storming their compound. But that wasn't very likely. "Use your best judgment."

"Got it," Walker said, pleased with the response.

"What about the sentries?" Yamashita asked from his overwatch vantage point.

"You'll take out the tower man on my signal," Cross said. Then he looked at Walker. "The Chief and I will deal with the ground lookouts before we split up. Yamashita, I'll signal you again when we're ready to take out the lights. Then I'll neutralize the guards on the longhouse to draw the others' attention."

Cross turned to face Walker. "When the pirates come running, that's your fireteam's cue," he said to Walker. "We'll regroup when you've got your side sewn up and Williams has confirmed that the hostages are safe."

Walker nodded.

"Everybody clear?" Cross asked.

"Hoorah," the squadron responded as one. They said it quietly, but with confidence.

Ever so slowly, Cross and Walker crawled on their bellies across the exposed ground toward the pirates' compound. The wet tropical heat was nearly unbearable. Insects Cross had never even heard of treated them like a buffet table. Within minutes, the two men were covered with itching bug bites.

But all the two men could do was ignore the discomfort. Any sudden or quick movements could result in a barrage of automatic rifle fire. The name of the game was patience.

After what seemed like an eternity, Walker and Cross crawled to within a dozen yards of the patrolling sentries without any alarm going off. The sentries looked at ease and relaxed. They had no idea what was coming.

With a twitch of his finger, Cross signaled Walker to halt. Behind them, Williams, Brighton, Shepherd, and Larssen all stopped as well. As the unaware sentries chatted with each other in Somali, Cross tightened his grip on his black tactical knife. Walker readied a well-used but razor-sharp KA-BAR blade that looked older than he was. When the sentries passed, Cross tapped his earphone twice, signaling Yamashita.

Then Cross popped up behind the sentries from his prone position. Walker sprang to his feet at the same time. Lightning quick, the two of them pounced on the sentries. Cross and Walker dragged their targets down, then silenced them with their blades. Quietly, carefully, they dragged their targets out of sight.

At the same moment, Lieutenant Yamashita squeezed off a single round from his M110 sniper rifle. The weapon's suppressor hid the muzzle flare and reduced the sound of the shot to a whisper. On the watchtower, the sentry sat down hard in the corner, then slumped over on his side.

"Tower clear," came Yamashita's voice through Cross's earpiece.

"Perimeter clear," Cross said, barely loud enough for the earphone to register. "Confirm?"

"Confirmed," Paxton, Yamashita's spotter, replied. "No one from the compound appears to be aware of our presence."

Cross and Walker nodded to each other as they cleaned their blades on the backs of the sentries' jackets. They returned their knives to their sheaths and then produced their suppressor-equipped M4 carbine rifles.

With Williams in tow, Cross moved parallel to the length of the pirate compound until the guards on the longhouse were cut off from sight. Meanwhile, Walker led Brighton, Shepherd, and Larssen in the opposite direction. They took up strategic positions around the pirates' mess and barracks. As the four of them got ready, Cross and Williams made their way around the darkened rear of the longhouse. They crept through the shadows toward the two men guarding the hostages. Cross moved inside first, keeping Williams hidden in the darkness.

Cross tapped his earphone, signaling Yamashita. "Ready, Commander," Yamashita's voice replied through the earpiece. "On your signal."

Cross took a deep breath. He tried to swallow down the excitement as adrenaline coursed through his veins. He took a second breath. Then a third. Centering himself, Cross crept up to the corner of the longhouse and tapped his earphone twice more to give Yamashita the signal. A split-second later, a pinpoint-accurate shot from Yamashita's rifle took out the outdoor light mounted on the face of the longhouse.

None of the pirates heard the shot itself, but the sound of the light fixture shattering into a million pieces definitely caught their attention. A second and third shot in quick succession took out the lights over the mess and barracks. The guards bolted up from their chairs waving their AK-47s back and forth wildly, trying to locate the threat. Other pirates nearby scrambled into frantic activity.

As pieces from the shattered lights rained down, Cross was already coming around the corner. One of the longhouse guards had his back to Cross.

A three-round burst from Cross's silenced carbine struck the pirate between his shoulder blades. The man fell dead into the arms of his compatriot. Their weapons were trapped between them for a crucial, fatal instant.

The second guard had heard the first set of muffled shots, but hadn't realized what was happening before his partner had collapsed. Cross opened fire with a second burst. The bullets caught the guard in the chest and dropped him lifeless to the ground. Neither man had so much as cocked his weapon.

Their deaths, however, hadn't gone unnoticed. The eight guards who remained at sea level saw the lights blow out, followed by a fully armed man darting into their midst from the darkness. Although caught off guard by the suddenness of the attack, they were at least well trained enough to react like soldiers rather than frightened rats. None of them had their AK-47s in hand, but several of them carried pistols strapped to their hips. Several pirates drew and raised them to open fire.

Bullets whizzed through the air, digging into the ground and splintering the wall of the longhouse all around Cross. But Cross hadn't stopped moving. He launched around a corner and dove for cover around the far side of the building. He rolled into a patch of shadow, but the startled pirates quickly closed in on his position.

Their quick and well-trained reactions, however, just put the pirates in more danger. They hadn't realized they were dealing with more than one man. As they advanced on Cross's position with weapons raised, Walker and his three-man team opened fire.

From the darkness, Brighton, Walker, and Larssen cut down the two pirates closest to Cross. As they stepped into the light from behind the barracks shadows, the soldiers came face-to-face with two unarmed pirates looking for cover. At the sight of Brighton's masked face and the barrel of his AA-12 combat shotgun, the pirates skidded gracelessly to a stop, then stumbled in the opposite direction. Brighton grinned. He hadn't even needed to pull the trigger — they were headed right where he wanted them.

At the same moment, Staff Sergeant Shepherd rose from prone position a dozen or so yards away. His bipod-mounted M240L machine gun had nothing to suppress the sound or flash as he opened fire.

The automatic weapon's roar frightened even the bravest of the pirates. Lucky for them, Shepherd didn't target any of the pirates specifically. He was using the thundering machine gun fire in order to corral them into the mess hall.

Shepherd stitched a few lines in the dirt around the couple of pirates who were still trying to return fire. The automatic fire drove those pirates back as well. Soon, all six remaining pirates had taken cover inside the mess hall.

One of the bravest of the pirates leaned out low with his pistol raised. He quickly squeezed off a couple of rounds at Brighton and Larssen as they approached the hatch near the center of the compound. The soldiers dove out of the way just as the shots bounced off the metal and concrete. Shepherd opened fire one more time, spraying the entire front of the mess with bullets. No one could tell if the pirate was hit or not, but he disappeared back inside and stopped firing.

Cross emerged from his cover position. "Hold fire!" he called out. Shepherd ceased fire at once. From within the longhouse came the sound of someone crying. Cross silently prayed that none of the bullets had hit any of the hostages inside — or his own men. "Anybody hit?"

"We're good," Brighton said as he and Larssen rose to their feet. Brighton wore a maniacal grin that was part adrenaline, part terror, and part relief.

Chief Walker emerged from the shadows. "All clear," he said calmly. His eyes and his M4 stayed focused on the single doorway leading out of the mess. "Form up."

There was no further aggression from inside the mess, but they could hear the six remaining pirates moving around inside. At least three of them were still armed, and none cried out as if seriously hurt.

"Sew them up, Chief," Cross said, nodding to Walker.

Walker returned the gesture and joined Brighton and Larssen in front of the mess building. In heavily accented Somali, he ordered the men inside to throw out their weapons and come out with their hands up. A lot of fast murmuring could be heard, but no weapons or pirates emerged. Walker repeated his demand in Arabic as Brighton and Larssen silently rushed to the door and took positions on opposite sides.

Walker waited. Again, he received no response. He approached the door and produced an M84 flashbang grenade from his belt. Larssen and Brighton nodded.

Walker pulled the pin on the grenade but kept the spoon down. "Last chance," he warned, his voice grim. He counted down slowly from five inside his head. At zero, seeing none of the pirates emerge, he shrugged.

The grenade clattered through the doorway. A bright flash exploded within. A second later, Larssen, Brighton, and Walker snaked into the building.

Cross turned toward the longhouse. With a tap on his earphone, he said, "Keep us covered, overwatch."

"Sir," Yamashita and Shepherd answered from their respective cover positions.

Cross approached the longhouse door to find Williams already there. He was carefully checking the bodies of the dead guards slumped over in the dark. After briefly fishing through one pirate's pockets, he produced a key to the longhouse. The corpsman handed it to Cross, who deftly opened the padlock on the door.

"Coming in," Cross said, pushing the door open. He led with his M4 just in case any pirates might be holed up inside with the hostages. Williams followed, equally alert.

There were no pirates inside the building. Only the terrified hostages they'd expected to find were present. Six men and two women were huddled in the back against the rear wall.

Cross thought there were supposed to be nine hostages, not eight. "Is anybody hurt?" he asked, lowering his M4.

The hostages looked back and forth at each other, then shook their heads. Some were still shivering. They were dirty and disheveled, and a few had bruises that looked to be a couple of days old.

"Clear," came Walker's report in Cross's earpiece. Larssen and Brighton echoed the sentiment.

"Well done," Cross replied to them all.

Williams slung his rifle over his shoulder and moved past Cross. "Got a man down over here," he said. The hostages parted, revealing a prone figure at the rear of the building. The man was a dirty and covered in bruises, cuts, and dried blood.

"Is he hit?" Cross asked, his voice heavy with concern.

"No," one of the hostages said, finding her voice. "They beat him. Every day, they hurt him for trying to call for help."

"It's Smithee," Williams said. He knelt beside the man and broke out his first-aid gear. "He's stable, but he's in bad shape. Let me patch him up and he'll be able to move in a little while."

"All right," Cross said. "Do what you can for him. We've only got a few minutes."

With a hand to his earphone, Cross stepped outside. He walked toward the hatch at the heart of the camp. "Overwatch, we're all clear here," Cross said. "Reel in."

Yamashita, Paxton, and Shepherd all acknowledged the order and began to head toward the rest of the team. Meanwhile, Brighton had emerged from the mess building, his combat shotgun held low and casual in front of him. He'd removed his night-vision goggles. He was all smiles as he came out, but the expression disappeared as he saw the dead pirates sprawled in the dirt between the buildings.

"The barracks is empty and the mess is all clear, Commander," Brighton reported, eyes still on the bodies. "Chief's talking to the pirates now."

"How many of them are still alive?" Cross asked.

"Five," Brighton said, making eye contact. "Shepherd iced the one taking shots at Larssen and me. The rest are fine."

"Which one is our so-called King of the Sea?" Cross asked.

"Malik al-Bahar?" Brighton asked. "The pirates were trying to say that the dead guy inside is him, but the Chief wasn't buying it." He shrugged.

"The Military Intelligence guys can sort all that out," Cross said. "Let's just make sure we get everybody." He pointed at the hatch. "Did they say what's down here?"

"Store rooms and their command center," Chief Walker said, emerging from the mess. "Beyond that is the dock in the cave down at the bottom."

"Any more pirates left?" Cross asked. "Other than the one guarding their boat, that is."

"They wouldn't say," Walker grumbled. "They're pretty disciplined, all things considered. They wanted me to believe their leader is dead already, but two of them pointed out different corpses before they got their story straight."

"Either you've got him in there —" Cross began.

"Or he's down the hole," Brighton finished.

"Or," Walker said, shooting Brighton an annoyed glance, "he's down the hole."

"Maybe I'll go help Williams with the hostages," Brighton suggested, backing away quickly. Brighton went over to the hostages and began speaking to them in friendly tones.

Shepherd arrived, lugging his machine gun. "The others are just behind me, Commander," he reported. "Should be here shortly."

"Looks like everything's squared away up here," Chief Walker said. Then he nodded at the hatch. "I'll take a couple of the boys down there and —"

"Negative," Cross cut in. "I want you to stay and see what else you can get from the prisoners. Your Somali's better than mine." In fact, Cross didn't speak Somali at all. "And make double sure we haven't missed anybody. I'll take two of you down with me to clean up and secure their boat. You get everybody up here ready to depart."

Walker's jaw line hardened. "It's your call," he said flatly. It was obvious that he wasn't happy about it, but orders were orders.

Brighton was busy showing off his combat shotgun to a couple of the hostages. They looked more nervous than impressed.

"I need you, Brighton," Cross called, waving him down. "You too," he told Larssen, as he spotted the Ranger herding five zip-cuffed Somali pirates out of the mess. Cross turned to Shepherd. "Take over. Keep them covered."

"Sir," Shepherd said. He grinned, hefting his M240L up as if to fire from the hip and spray the pirates at the first sign of provocation. It was a terrible firing posture, but the pirates were still intimidated. Taking his cue, Chief Walker barked at the pirates to sit. The men practically threw themselves on the ground trying to comply.

"What are the orders, sir?" Larssen asked.

"We're going down the hole," Cross said.

Cross reached down for the hatch. It was roughly twenty inches in diameter and opened easily. Inside, a metal shaft shot straight down into darkness. The top of the narrow ladder could be seen a few feet from the opening.

Cross nodded at Brighton. He went first, holding out his AA-12, muzzle down, in case they met any resistance while bottled up on the ladder. Cross went second, and Larssen brought up the rear. The cool air was a brief relief from the heat and humidity topside.

They made it down without incident to find a cinder-block storeroom full of food and medical supplies. It wasn't clear whether it belonged to the recently captured World Food Program vessel or was simply part of the pirates' private supply.

"This seems rather well stocked for a tiny island in the middle of nowhere," Lieutenant Larssen said.

"Piracy's good business, man," Brighton said. "And this al-Bahar guy's been hiding out here for years. He's had plenty of time to do all this. I'm surprised it's not more built up."

Without offering his own opinion, Cross put a finger to his lips, then pointed at the door that led out of the room. The soldiers took the hint and silently moved out the door into a short hallway. Cross stepped across the hall and found a second storeroom as big as the first. Rather than food and medicine, however, this storeroom was full of crates of weapons and ammunition. They were mostly AK-47s, although there were several RPG-7s, too. Automatic pistols, Soviet-era hand grenades, and C-4 plastic explosive rounded out the rest of the inventory.

Brighton's eyes went wide. "Good thing we caught them with their guard down," he said.

Cross nodded soberly. He was troubled by the sheer volume of firepower present in the storeroom. There were more weapons here than the pirates they'd killed and captured above could possibly ever use. Why did they have so much? Was it just a stockpile, or was there an army of pirates they had yet to encounter? The mess and barracks up top were suitable for the small numbers they'd seen. But maybe the Shayatin al-Bahar were trying to turn their island hideaway into some sort of resupply station for more pirate bands than just their own.

No use in trying to guess, Cross decided. He signaled for his fireteam to move out. They stepped out of the storeroom and turned left, continuing down the hall.

At the end of the hallway was a much smaller room crammed with fans, flat-screen monitors, and surprisingly high-end computers. The monitors were all asleep and the computers were in power-saving mode. However, as they entered the room, a cheap motion-sensor in the ceiling brought the machines to life.

Images of the shipping lanes through the Indian Ocean and Arabian Sea dominated the monitors. Differently colored dots — likely representing the different ships — blinked and moved slowly along the white lines that represented shipping lanes.

"Wow," Cross said. He turned to Brighton. "I want this. All of it. Start copying files and . . . tracing IPs . . . or whatever."

Brighton cocked an eyebrow, but managed to refrain from laughing in Cross's face. Cross would be the first to admit he was no computer genius.

"How about I pull the hard drives, Commander?" Brighton offered diplomatically.

"Go for it," Cross said. Brighton plopped down in the chair to shut the computers down.

Cross turned to Larssen. "Let's head back to the armory and start setting the explosives," he said. "I don't want anybody to recover those weapons after we're gone."

"Sir," Larssen said eagerly. He turned in place as Cross joined him, but suddenly flinched back.

A man stood at the other end of the hallway, pointing an AK-47 into the room. His eyes met Cross's just as Cross realized he was there.

All in the same second, Cross raised his M4, Larssen shoved Cross aside with one hand, and the furious man opened fire with his AK-47.

Despite the snarl of rage on his face, the man fired with control. He put a single shot into Larssen's chest and a second into Brighton's back. Cross stumbled into a low table at Larssen's shove.

By the time Cross had regained his balance, the shooter was rushing down the hall. The pirate's automatic rifle was low and at the ready. Cross took cover behind the door frame and fired a couple of shots down the hall. He just missed the

pirate gunman as the man dove into the weapons storeroom for cover.

Brighton gasped, groggy and breathless. He pushed himself up off the desk. "Which one of y'all just shot me?" he said.

Cross hated to take his eyes off the hallway, but he spared a quick glance at his men. Neither Larssen nor Brighton was seriously injured thanks to their ballistic armor, though they'd be feeling every bruise and cracked rib in the morning. Larssen was still gasping from having the wind knocked out of him, but there was no permanent damage. Cross didn't even see any blood.

"Keep working on the computer," Cross told Brighton. The sergeant nodded but shook his head a few times to clear it.

Cross looked to Larssen next. "Lieutenant, are you —"

Larssen nodded, looking more annoyed than injured. Like Cross, Larssen knew that leaving the pirate alone in that armory was one of the worst things they could do. "Go," Larssen croaked, finally getting his wind back. He struggled to stand. "I'm right behind you."

"No, cover Brighton," Cross said firmly. "I'll be right back."

Cross drew out an M84 flashbang and removed the pin. He peeked out into the hall, hoping to surprise the pirate before the man had a chance to dig out one of the more lethal fragmentation grenades from the armory. If the pirate chucked one of those down the hall, Cross and his men were done for. But as Cross spied out the doorway, he saw that the pirate hadn't realized his advantage. Instead of picking up a grenade, he'd opted for grabbing a second AK-47. He was emerging from the armory with a machine gun tucked under each arm like an action movie hero.

The pirate hustled backward toward the door at the far end of the hallway. When he saw Cross peek around the door, the man opened fire with both guns, filling the hall with flying lead.

Most of the shots went wide from the less-than-stable double firing positions, but Cross ducked back reflexively anyway. Without looking, Cross flung his flashbang over his shoulder and down the hall.

The burst disoriented the gunman and put a stop to his wild spray of fire. It didn't do enough to incapacitate him, though, as he bumped and staggered the rest of the way to the far door. Although he had to drop one of the machine guns to do it, he pulled the door open and fled.

Cross threw one last glance to confirm that Brighton and Larssen were okay. Then he charged out the door in pursuit of his prey.

Cross expected machine gun fire to greet him as he exited the room. However, all he found was a discarded empty magazine, indicating that the pirate had at least reloaded before moving on.

Cross moved quickly, his eyes darting left and right. Ahead of him lay a stone stairway that zigzagged down through the island's interior. Cross peeked down through the central stairwell. The pirate's running footsteps echoed up from the bottom.

Cross only saw the pirate's shadow when the man reached the bottom level. However, the shadow passed out of sight before Cross could even think to throw a second flashbang.

There was no option but to plunge ahead after him.

Cross broke into a controlled sprint. "Overwatch!" he said with a tap on his earphone. "I'm flushing a hostile out the bottom of the cliff! Tell me if he tries to make for the sea!"

"Sir," Yamashita answered calmly.

Running as fast as he could while keeping his breathing calm, Cross reached the bottom of the stairs. An open doorway was between him and his prey.

Cross resisted the instinct to just barrel through the door and continue the chase. Instead, he kicked it open from the side, then immediately took cover behind the wall next to the doorframe.

That flash of caution saved Cross, as the fleeing pirate had been waiting a dozen feet back for Cross to appear. With a shouted curse in Somali, the pirate opened fire the moment the door swung open.

Bullet by bullet, a full clip of ammo ripped into the walls and the stairs behind Cross. The pirate kept firing at full auto until his AK-47 finally clipped out.

At that moment, Cross popped around the corner.

Cross shot back in the direction where he thought the pirate would be. The bullet hit the pirate in the arm. Cross saw the pirate drop his rifle and turn to flee.

As Cross gave chase, he realized he'd emerged into a cave that had to be somewhere near sea level. Electric generators, tools, and barrels of fuel filled half the space. Cross could hear the sound of the ocean in the direction he was running, as well as the revving of a boat engine.

Cross picked up speed as he exited the mouth of the cave. It led into a much broader cave that opened directly to the sea. A metal catwalk ran to a dock where the pirates' mother ship was just beginning to pull away.

The pirate Cross had been chasing clung to a metal ladder on the side of the moving ship. He was desperately trying to clamber aboard with one wounded arm. Cross had no time to consider his options. In one deft movement, he dropped his nearly empty M4 on the catwalk and drew his SIG P226 from his holster.

Picking up speed, Cross dashed down the length of the dock. Running at a full sprint, he leapt just as the boat's pilot gunned the engine.

Cross's outstretched arm caught one of the rungs of the ladder as the boat pulled away. He tightened his grip and looked up to see the wounded pirate disappear over the edge of the boat, onto the deck.

Cross struggled upward after him. He climbed one-handed, his pistol pointed up in case the pirate popped over the side with a weapon. Cross made it up near the deck just as the boat was clearing the cave.

When Cross reached the top, he glanced over the edge. There he saw not only the pirate he'd been chasing, but another one who had gone unaccounted for during their initial recon sweep.

The second pirate stood waiting for Cross with a grim smile — and a loaded AK-47.

"Drop the pistol," the wounded pirate said in thickly accented English.

Cross slowly raised the pistol, then tossed it over his shoulder into the sea. As he did, he made sure that his thumb brushed past the inside of his earphone.

"All right," Cross said, speaking slowly. "I'm climbing up onboard. Don't shoot me."

"Not yet," the pirate agreed with an amused smirk. He kept his gun trained on Cross as he slowly climbed over the edge and onto the deck. Now that he wasn't running for his life, the pirate sounded almost jovial — if a little winded. "Not until I've properly punished you for what you have done to —"

"Okay," Cross said, looking the armed pirate in the eyes. "Now shoot."

The gunman frowned in confusion. He glanced at the wounded man beside him. A small red light shone brightly on the gunman's forehead.

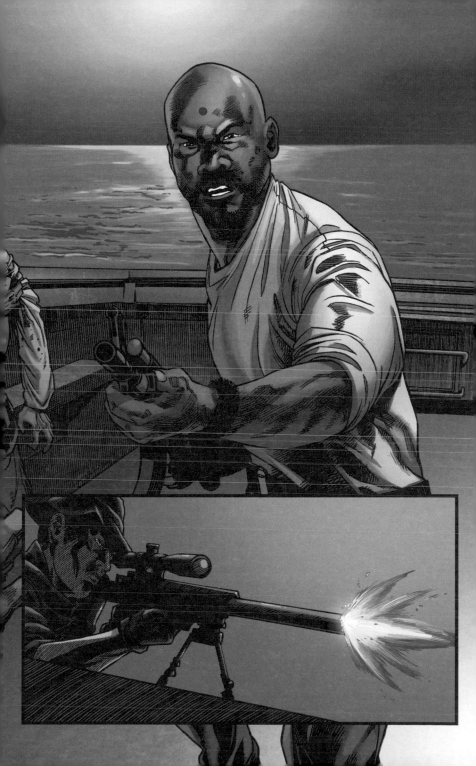

A moment later, the pirate crumpled to the deck like an empty sack.

"Thank you," Cross said.

"Sir," Yamashita said through Cross's earpiece. His tone was as calm and unemotional as ever.

Cross walked over and picked up the dead man's rifle as the second pirate gaped at him shock. "Now," Cross told him, "why don't you introduce me to your pilot?"

* * *

An hour later, the morning sun was inching its way above the horizon. Everyone from the island was boarded onto the pirates' mother ship. The seven pirates who had survived the raid, including the boat's pilot, were zip-cuffed and bound together on the aft deck. The World Food Program hostages, Staff Sergeant Brighton, Second Lieutenant Larssen, and Alan Smithee's cameraman were all below deck either eating in the galley or recovering in the pirates' quarters.

Alan Smithee, heavily bandaged, paced the deck while staring out at the gray waves of the Indian Ocean. He loudly bemoaned the loss of his cameras, and remarked to anyone within hearing distance about his new big-budget action film that would tell the story of his capture and rescue.

Cross had taken the helm of the ship. He steered it out to sea to link up with one of the Navy's warships on patrol in the area. He reasoned that would be faster than waiting for command to send someone to pick everyone up as he'd originally planned.

Chief Walker had been on the radio since the ship left dock, reporting in and arranging the rendezvous. After the last outgoing transmission, for fifteen minutes, Walker didn't say a word to Cross. Neither did he leave, though, which implied he had something on his mind.

After another ten minutes of silence, Walker finally spoke up. "I have to admit," he said. "You ran a good, clean op, despite how little we knew before we touched ground. No team casualties, all hostages accounted for . . . I'm impressed."

Cross took a moment to gather his thoughts. He kept his gaze straight ahead, away from Walker. "Golly, thanks, Chief," he said, faking a tone of childlike wonder. "That makes it all worthwhile."

Then Cross looked at Walker and grinned. The Chief relaxed a little but still did a fine job of looking annoyed. Walker turned on his heel and left the wheelhouse grumbling in Spanish, "*Ese idiota. ¿Por qué intentarlo?*"

Walker slammed the door. Only then did Cross permit himself a soft chuckle at his second-in-command's expense. All things considered, though, Walker was right. Things had gone well. But Cross knew it wasn't always going to be that way. Sometimes the bad guys won, despite the good guys doing everything right.

But for now, Cross was content in the knowledge that he'd done well. There was no doubt in Cross's mind that the feeling wouldn't last long, but it would do for now.

"Until the next one," Cross said softly. "Hoorah."

MISSION DEBRIEFING

OPERATION

SEA DEMON 1234

MISSION COMPLETE

PRIMARY OBJECTIVE

- Secure hostages and transport them to safety

SECONDARY OBJECTIVES

- Neutralize all enemy combatants while minimizing loss of life

- Identify possible leads in preventing future attacks by pirates

STATUS

3/3 COMPLETE

3245.98 ● ● ●

CROSS, RYAN

RANK: Lieutenant Commander
BRANCH: Navy SEAL
PSYCH PROFILE: Team leader of Shadow Squadron. Control oriented and loyal, Cross insisted on hand-picking each member of his squad.

The mission went smoothly. All hostages were recovered without harm, all hostiles were neutralized with minimal force, and steps are being taken to ensure that these self-proclaimed "Sea Demons" remain landlocked for the foreseeable future.

All in all, I'd say Shadow Squadron's inaugural mission was a complete and total success.

— Lieutenant Commander Ryan Cross

ERROR

UNAUTHORIZED

USER MUST HAVE LEVEL 12 CLEARANCE
OR HIGHER IN ORDER TO GAIN ACCESS
TO FURTHER MISSION INFORMATION.

2019.681

LOADING MISSION:

BLACK ANCHOR

3245.98 ● ● ●

1216.062

2012.241

MISSION BRIEFING

OPERATION

BLACK ANCHOR 1234

A Chinese oil rig platform in Cuban waters has been hijacked by unknown forces, and they've taken the workers hostage. The Cuban military is on its way, and they have no concern for the lives of anyone on board. The Chinese military will intervene in short order, as well.

In order to avoid a messy international incident. we need to get in, get the hostages, neutralize the hostiles, and get out. Fast.

— Chief Petty Officer Alonso Walker

3245.98

GULF OF MEXICO

PRIMARY OBJECTIVE

- Secure the oil rig platform and transport hostages to safety

SECONDARY OBJECTIVES

- Minimize damage done to Hardwall mercenaries

- Avoid contact with the Cuban and Chinese forces

1932.789

0412.981

1624.054

BLACK
ANCHOR

The black salt water engulfed Chief Petty Officer Alonso Walker on all sides. He was in his element — both literally and figuratively. As a child, Walker had believed that the black depths of the ocean were filled with giant monsters like the Kraken, the Leviathan, and Moby Dick. But now, as an adult, Walker knew there were few creatures in the sea more dangerous than himself. After all, he had been an elite career soldier of the US Navy.

Now he was second-in-command of Shadow Squadron. His present state had been a long time in the making. After coasting through twelve years of school with near-perfect grades, Walker shocked his friends and family by enlisting in the Navy the day after graduation.

From the beginning, Walker had his sights set on joining the legendary SEALs. After a grueling trip through the SEAL training program, he'd earned himself a place on Team Two based out of Little Creek, Virginia. He served with distinction through multiple tours, climbing up the ranks and piling up the medals. And making the world a better, safer place in the best way he knew how.

In time, his skillful and honorable service caught the Joint Special Operations Command's attention. Officers there selected Walker for inclusion in Shadow Squadron. For several years now, he'd traveled throughout the world to perform top secret black ops against nothing less than the forces of evil. Walker was probably too old to think of his job in such corny terms, but in his heart he still believed in the righteousness of the work he did. And he believed that if his friends and family back home knew about the work he did, they'd be quite proud of him.

But if they saw him here and now, floating in these frigid, black waters, Walker wondered if his loved ones would be worried about him.

Walker was in the early stages of a mission, floating alongside the mighty *USS Georgia.* It loomed in the water like one of the imaginary monsters of Walker's childhood. But here in the otherwise empty darkness, Walker found the sub's presence to be comforting, not frightening.

Sucking recycled air through his rebreather, Walker kick-stroked to the rear of the bullet-shaped dry deck shelter near the *Georgia.* The DDS's circular rear hatch stood open. At the moment, four of his teammates were carefully sliding a black, torpedo-shaped vessel out into the ocean.

The vessel was a swimmer delivery vehicle, though SEALs like Walker preferred to think of them as SEAL delivery vehicles. It served as an open submersible that could carry up to eight soldiers undetected. The SDV could travel distances greater than any person could reasonably be expected to swim, especially in frigid ocean waters. Walker had trained on SDVs for as long as he'd been a SEAL, and he and his fellow SDV soldiers secretly considered themselves to be a cut above even their "vanilla" SEAL brethren.

While Walker was no slouch at land navigation or airborne insertion, he was most at home in the water. He'd worked hard to see that every man on Shadow Squadron — especially those who'd come from the Army, Marines, and Air Force — completed their combat swimmer training with only the highest marks. He was still undoubtedly the best and most experienced combat swimmer on the unit, but he had total faith in his men's capabilities beneath the waves.

Of course, they weren't really his men, he had to admit. The JSOC had seen fit to recruit and saddle him with a new commanding officer: Lieutenant Commander Ryan Cross.

It rankled Walker. Cross hadn't been in the Navy as long as he had. Cross hadn't been a SEAL as long as he had. Cross had combat experience, but not as much as Walker had. And worst of all, Cross wasn't even an SDV SEAL — he was pure "vanilla" SEAL. Before being recruited into Shadow Squadron, Cross had done more mountaineering and arctic survival training than SDV training.

So why did the JSOC put this man in charge of Shadow Squadron? Walker wondered.

On the positive side, Cross did run a clean op. Shadow Squadron hadn't lost a single man — so far. They'd faced pirates off the Somali coast, accomplishing their mission with slick professionalism and impressive flexibility. Walker worried, though, that their early successes might go to Cross's head.

Cross had come to Shadow Squadron with a reputation as a hero and a natural leader. In Walker's experience, that almost always went hand in hand with stubbornness and over-confidence. So far, the lieutenant commander listened to input, and he suffered disagreement pretty well, but he was quick to halt discussion when he felt his point had been proven.

True, Walker probably could argue with his CO a little less, but the man just seemed too smug. It was hard not to want to put him in his place once in a while. But Commander Cross was right more often than he was wrong. That only made him all the more annoying.

Thankfully, Walker's sense of professionalism ensured that he put his feelings aside when the team was in the field. The men needed to see unity in their ranks. If he, the second-in-command, was always second-guessing and arguing with Cross, it would unsettle the others. A lack of focus would likely end up getting someone killed. So no matter what he thought of Lieutenant Commander Cross personally, Walker knew he wouldn't be able to continue his service with another man's death on his conscience.

But that didn't mean Walker had to keep his opinions to himself *before* Shadow Squadron's missions got underway . . .

* * *

Earlier that day, at dawn, Cross gathered his eight-man Shadow Squadron unit in the base ready room. The smell of fresh coffee hung thick in the air as all the other well-groomed men wearing camouflage fatigues shook off the morning weariness.

Cross, on the other hand, seemed to have plenty of energy. It was just one more reason for Walker to dislike him: Cross was a morning person.

"We've got another situation," Cross said energetically. He tapped on the computer-operated whiteboard on the wall and synced up with the room's tablet computer. "And this one hits pretty close to home."

That got the men's attention. Ever since the events of 9/11, the fear of further terrorist action on American soil had loomed large over the nation. None were more sensitive to the terrorist threat than those in the military.

Cross brought up a satellite map of the Gulf of Mexico, focusing on its eastern half. "I'm sure you're all familiar with the problems brewing in the waters just off Cuba," he said.

Walker knew what Cross was referring to, but a quick glance at the other men made it clear that they didn't.

Staff Sergeant Edgar Brighton raised his hand. "Sorry, Commander," he said, not looking sorry at all. "I get all my news from Jon Stewart and Stephen Colbert."

A few chuckles came from the other men. Walker glared at the young man, shaming Brighton and silencing the others. Walker thought that Brighton's class clown act was getting a little old. It was unbecoming conduct for an elite soldier.

"Sorry, Chief Walker," Brighton mumbled, having the decency to at least look embarrassed. He turned back to face Cross. "All the same, I'm still not quite sure what you're referring to, sir."

"It's all right," Cross said, taking it far too easy on Brighton for Walker's tastes.

Walker frowned. *If Cross doesn't start making an example out of Brighton,* Walker thought, *the other men will start thinking it's okay to be so casual.*

Cross tapped and swiped on the tablet computer, bringing up an overlay on the whiteboard. Green and yellow zones showed up surrounding the coasts of the United States and Cuba. A blue zone appeared over the coast of Mexico. A roughly triangular gap appeared in the Gulf where the three zones didn't quite reach one another.

"For a few years now," Cross said, "the Chinese government has been negotiating with what's left of the Castro regime in Cuba for rights to drill for oil and natural gas in Cuba's territorial waters. Last month, Cuba agreed, and China set up its Hēi Máo gas and oil platform in the eastern Gulf of Mexico."

"Hēi Máo means Black Anchor in the Chinese language," Walker added.

Cross nodded, then tapped his tablet again. A red dot appeared in the northwestern part of the yellow zone with the words *Black Anchor* above it. Cross pointed at the red dot that was right next to the triangular gap. "It's Cuba's right to choose who they share their resources with, but their zone is right next to our country's zone," he said. "For some folks in Congress, having the Chinese float a GOPLAT in the Gulf at all makes them . . . uneasy."

That's an understatement, Walker thought. There was an awful lot of oil and natural gas buried beneath the Gulf of Mexico, but not every source was partitioned neatly. Quite often, more than one country had access to a reserve, causing tension between nations. Even worse, sometimes oil sources overlapped boundaries. That was a negotiations nightmare for all the countries involved.

"I can't say I'm too thrilled about the situation either, Commander," Walker said.

"Normally, this sort of thing is handled by the suits in Washington," Cross said, "But then yesterday, something happened."

With another swipe across his tablet, the red dot on the whiteboard drifted northward. When the red dot crossed into the triangular region on the map, it vanished. "Yesterday the Black Anchor drifted into this doughnut hole here, then went dark."

A glance around gave Walker the impression that Cross's supposedly dramatic comment had just left the men even more confused.

Walker stood up, taking it upon himself to clarify the situation. "The 'doughnut hole' is the spot between where the exclusive economic zones offshore of the United Stats, Mexico, and Cuba don't quite meet up together," he explained. "Arguing over ownership of the doughnut hole has been relatively quiet until China and Cuba started fighting over it recently."

"So how did this GOPLAT get installed there?" Brighton asked.

"It's not a fixed platform," Walker answered before Cross could. "It's a floating oil rig. It's supposed to be held in place by a set of anchors, but if the anchors are up, it can move around freely. That's part of the reason Congress put so much pressure on the president to raise a fuss when the Chinese put the Black Anchor where they did. They figured it was just a matter of time before the platform 'accidentally' ended up in the doughnut hole. Looks like Congress was right."

"Sounds like the president has a doughnut hole in his head," Brighton joked.

"That's your government you're talking about," Walker said sharply. "Show some respect."

"Sorry, Chief," Brighton said. He looked at Cross, as if seeking support but Walker was pleased to see that Cross looked rather peeved at the young man, as well.

Brighton sat up straight. He added, "So when you say this thing went dark, Commander, I'm guessing it didn't really disappear."

"Nope," Cross said, changing the whiteboard display once more. It now showed an ocean-level view of the Chinese GOPLAT, as seen from several miles away. A set of map coordinates and a time stamp from the previous day appeared in the corner of the screen. The platform looked like an array of metal scaffoldings with a huge crane on top. "We know exactly where it is — that isn't the problem. The Black Anchor radioed for resupply early last week, but ever since the resupply vessel came and went, all communication ceased."

"Do we know what happened?" Walker asked. He was still standing at the front of the ready room next to Cross.

"We didn't know until last night," Cross replied. "Shortly after the resupply vessel left, an unmarked speedboat showed up. It moored to the rig without permission and a team of armed men climbed aboard. They stormed the rig and took the crew hostage."

"Pirates again?" Brighton said. "I didn't even know the Gulf had pirates."

"They're not pirates," Cross said, his tone growing grim. "They're American mercenaries."

That statement blew away the last of the morning haze in the men. Their eyes grew wide and alert now. Cross tapped his computer tablet once more, bringing up a file photo of a square-jawed blond man in his thirties. Below the picture was a corporate logo for an American company called Hardwall Security.

"This is Corbin Van Sant," Cross said. "He and the attackers are private security contractors employed by Hardwall. The company's website claims they specialize in providing security at sea all around the world. Their 'onboard security experts' get paid to ride along with merchant vessels or escort ships to protect clients from pirates and other criminals. They also occasionally patrol the coastlines at home for what they call 'unwelcome visitors.'"

"Like the vigilantes along the border between the US and Mexico," said Mark Shepherd.

"Except these guys are highly trained and efficient," Cross said.

"In other words, dangerous," said Walker.

Cross nodded. "They made headlines a few years ago for exposing a South American drug-smuggling operation," he said. "But they spend most of their time searching for boats transporting illegal immigrants. The company's founder, Corbin Van Sant, has a reputation for a tough anti-immigration stance. He seems to think it's his personal mission to 'protect the sanctity of America's borders and waters.'"

"Sounds like a racist," one of the men mumbled. Walker saw it was Second Lieutenant Neil Larssen.

"So what happened, exactly?" Walker asked, redirecting the conversation. The more interruptions Cross allowed, the further off track this briefing would get. "This Corbin Van Sant character just suddenly decided to go from American patriot to international pirate?"

"Specifics are sketchy," Cross said. "What we know so far is that Van Sant had one of his boats watching the Black Anchor. He sent it over the second the platform left Cuba's waters. His men probably tried to intimidate the Chinese into going back the way they came, and when the Chinese refused, things got out of hand. Now we have a hostage situation. We don't know any other details, though. For all I know, Van Sant's guys came to the platform with every intention of hijacking it."

"How do we know this much in the first place, sir?" asked Yamashita. The stoic Army Ranger rarely spoke during mission briefings, which Walker appreciated, but something about this mission had apparently piqued his curiosity. "Have the Cubans asked us for help resolving it? Or the Chinese?"

"No," Cross admitted. "The Chinese argue that the doughnut hole in the gulf is in international waters. They believe they're within their rights. We only learned what we know from —"

"Spying?" Yamashita interrupted. He said it in a flat tone, without judgment.

"Yep," Cross confirmed. "Now, obviously, American citizens taking Chinese and Cuban nationals hostage is a big problem. Everybody's trying to keep it out of the news for now, but that's only going to be in the victims' best interests for so long. When the press gets wind of this, the United States is going to end up looking bad. The Chinese and Cubans are trying to negotiate with Van Sant's people, but we believe they're just stalling until they can mount a rescue operation. When they do, we'll be facing a major international incident."

"Not that we aren't already," Walker put in.

"Which is where we come in," Cross said. "We're going to board the Black Anchor before anyone else can, free those prisoners, and deal with the Hardwall mercenaries who took them hostage."

"Deal with them?" Brighton asked. "You mean like . . ." He pointed his finger to his temple.

"I'm hoping it doesn't come to that," Cross said.

"With all due respect," Walker said, "these are American citizens we're talking about."

"They are criminals," Cross said.

"American criminals, sir," Walker added. "We should make every effort to capture them alive so they can stand trial."

"These men are terrorizing foreign nationals in the name of one man's political agenda," Cross said. "They're an embarrassment to what our country stands for. If they force our hand, I will not make it easy for them."

"All the same —"Walker began.

"This isn't a discussion, Chief," Cross said sternly. "Now sit down. We have some work to do."

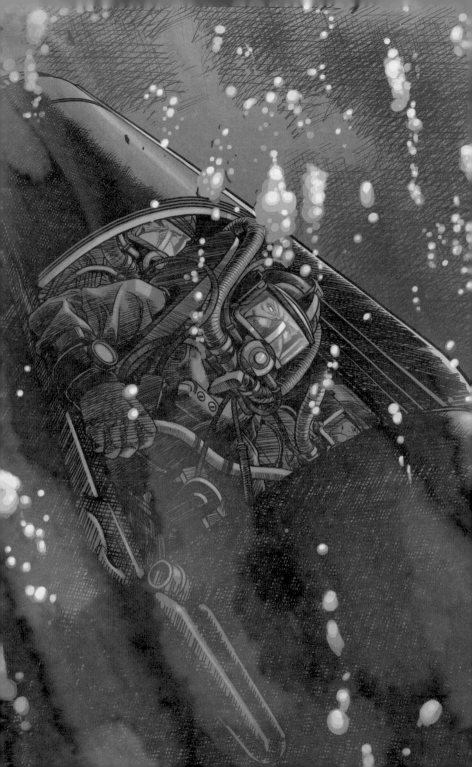

* * *

Walker's pride still stung as they traveled in the SDV. He wasn't normally the type to sulk, and he was disappointed in himself for not just shrugging it off and carrying on as normal.

But now wasn't the time to for brooding. From here on out, floating in the moonlit waters, the team was on noise discipline until the hostages and mercenaries were seen to. After that, Walker would figure out a way to tell his senior officer what he really thought of him.

But that just made the long, silent trip toward the Black Anchor feel even longer.

As the SDV glided through the water carrying its six combat swimmers, Chief Walker piloted the vehicle while Cross sat beside him, navigating by GPS and SONAR. The instruments gave off the only visible light.

In the rear compartment sat Brighton, Larssen, Yamashita, and Hospital Corpsman Second Class Kyle Williams. All six men sat in nearly total darkness, breathing on regulators attached to the SDV's onboard air tanks.

An SDV insertion wasn't ideal for an assault on a gas-and-oil platform. Fast-roping down from a hovering helicopter would have suited better. But stealth was a much higher priority than speed this time out.

It wasn't the hostiles the team had to worry about as much as the Cuban patrol boats around the Black Anchor. If one of those crafts spotted them sneaking in, they might assume the wrong thing — that the US government was trying to sneak out the Hardwall mercenaries. That would almost certainly lead to hostility.

So the team had chosen the SDV approach, which filled Walker with quiet satisfaction. Cross had initially argued for a fast-rope in, then for the Zodiac, almost as if he were afraid of using an SDV. Patiently, and with respect, Walker had poked holes in each of Cross's suggestions for insertion until the SDV was the only option left.

To be fair, Cross was qualified for SDV operations and he was a skilled navigator. However, Walker couldn't help but assume Cross was squirming with discomfort the whole time. And considering how far away in US waters they'd had to launch the SDV to avoid detection, it was an awful long time indeed.

Eventually, the Black Anchor platform showed up on the instruments. With practiced precision, Walker maneuvered the SDV alongside the submerged structure. Then he cut the engines.

Walker nodded to Cross. Cross killed the instrumentation lights and hit the release to open the doors. The pair of them switched from the SDV's air supply to their own rebreathers. Then, still deep beneath the surface of the water, Walker and Cross exited the vehicle. Behind them, Brighton, Larssen, Yamashita, and Williams emerged. While Cross moored the SDV to the Black Anchor, the others gently kick-stroked upward alongside it, taking great care to ascend slowly and silently.

Large blue and white LEDs dotted the outside of the tubes. They provided just enough illumination in the nighttime sea to lend the entire platform an alien appearance. Staring up at the overwhelming size of the rig, Walker could find no better word for it than amazing.

The underside of the Black Anchor consisted of six sealed vertical tubes wound around a seventh center tube. The tubes were hollow and allowed the rig to float or sink, depending on when the crew flushed or filled them with sea water.

Walker glanced at the set of four thick anchor chains that extended out into the darkness. It appeared that the crew had not been given a chance to extend the platform's drilling apparatus before the Hardwall mercenaries arrived.

Once Cross had finished securing the SDV, he signaled to Walker that it was time to go. The pair of them followed the other four men up. They rose together at a leisurely pace so they didn't decompress too quickly. If they didn't pace themselves, then nitrogen bubbles would expand rapidly in their bloodstream, giving them decompression sickness. That would bring a quick end to the mission — and probably their lives.

Fortunately, the sea was relatively calm, so they didn't have to fight strong currents to stay on course.

As they neared the surface, they found steel emergency ladders running up the outside of the tubes. Cross took the lead, swimming over to the nearest ladder. He ascended to just below the surface of the water, then stopped to look back at his men. They spread out below Cross so they could all see him. Walker could practically feel their excitement electrifying the water around them.

Cross's first signal was for total noise discipline. It was pointless underwater, but vital topside. If they lost the element of surprise against the mercenary hostiles, the hostages would likely be the ones to suffer for it.

Next Cross set the climbing order. He would go first, followed by Walker, Brighton, Yamashita, then Williams. Larssen would take the rear.

When the swimmers finished shuffling their positions in the water, Cross held up one hand as if he were holding an invisible tennis ball. It wasn't a standard military hand signal, but a reminder of a certain point Cross had relentlessly driven into their heads throughout training: *think spherically.*

It was a vital concept, especially on a structure like this. Incoming attacks wouldn't be restricted to just the front and rear as on a normal battlefield. On this rig, with so many levels, enemies could just as easily attack from above or below, so the men had to be ready for trouble to come at them from every direction. Spherically.

Cross had repeated the concept constantly in training, making the hand signal every single time. *Think spherically, think spherically, think spherically.* It was solid advice, even if the repetition had gotten on Walker's nerves long ago.

Finally, Cross nodded to his men, looped an elbow around the ladder, and begin to remove his diving fins. The other five soldiers got in order below and did likewise, tucking the fins on their backs under the straps that held their small complement of gear. When his booted feet were free, Cross began the long climb upward. The squad followed.

When Walker broke the surface, his sense of weight suddenly returned, as if he were an astronaut coming back from a long journey in space. Now he felt every pound of his gear, though he tried not to let it slow him down. A stiff breeze chilled the water on his hands and face, and the gentle muffling of sound beneath the waves was replaced by the harsh splash and crash of the waves below.

Under the full moon's light, Walker could now see much farther. The improved view showed him the Cuban patrol boats waiting in the distance for their chance to close in and turn this mission into a total mess.

Cuba's naval fleet wasn't all that impressive compared to America's modern ships, but it could still do plenty of damage. Intel indicated that at least one Chinese vessel was nearby as well, though Walker couldn't see well enough to pick it out. But he did identify the mercenaries' boat moored on the other side of the platform.

If things went according to plan, it wouldn't matter how many boats were out on the water, or where they were located. But Walker knew that few plans remained intact after first contact with the enemy. Adaptation was almost a certainty in missions. Van Sant's men could certainly testify to that — that is, if they hadn't come planning to take hostages in the first place.

After a short climb, Cross reached the top of the ladder, coming to the underside of a metal catwalk. He suddenly gave the stop signal, and Walker passed it down even though he wasn't sure what the holdup was. He got his answer a moment later as a mercenary strolled by on a long, lonely patrol of the catwalk.

This particular metal walkway was the lowest level on the platform that was still above water. The single sentry had likely been stationed down here to watch for boats trying to sneak people on board.

Walker smiled. Cross had to realize that if he'd had his way and inserted via Zodiac instead of SDV, this sentry would have seen them and raised the alarm. Or worse, the mercs would have waited until they boarded and then cut them down on the ladder as they climbed up. But because they'd done things Walker's way, the team had remained undetected — and gained the safety of the shadows beneath the walkway.

The sentry wore black fatigues, combat boots, and a Bluetooth earpiece. Slung around his shoulder was a Heckler & Koch MP5A3 submachine gun. A ballistic vest covered his broad chest. As he paced, his eyes remained focused on the thrashing waters below, hoping to spot and prevent any attempted insertions — like the one Shadow Squadron had just successfully performed.

The sentry continued his circuit, passing by the ladder where Cross's team waited below. He was entirely unaware of their presence. As the sentry passed, Cross signaled to Walker.

Quietly, Cross snuck up behind the mercenary with Walker on his heels. As soon as they reached the walkway, Cross rushed up behind the guard and slapped a choke hold around his neck. Cross's muscles tightened. He squeezed the man's pulsing arteries closed. Then Cross pulled the sentry to his knees, his weight pulling the man backward.

The mercenary tried to reach for his submachine gun hanging around his shoulder, but Walker cut the gun strap using his knife and took the weapon from the merc. He casually pitched it over the side of the safety rail and into the ocean.

Unable to shout for help, and growing weaker from the lack of blood flow to his brain, the sentry flailed wildly. Cross took the blows, patiently waiting for the sentry to slip into unconsciousness. Finally, the merc's eyes slowly slipped shut and he slumped into Cross's arms.

Cross carefully laid him on the catwalk. He checked his pulse, then nodded at Walker. Together, they flipped the merc over onto his belly.

Cross kept a lookout while Walker produced a pair of plastic zip ties from his pocket, then secured the man's hands behind his back. After that, he secured one ankle to the metal walkway rail. A quick search revealed the man had no other weapons or ID of any sort. Walker pitched the man's Bluetooth headset into the water below. Only then did Cross signal for the rest of the team to come up the ladder to the walkway.

Brighton, Yamashita, Williams, and Larssen climbed the walkway, then took their positions. Williams checked the

downed mercenary. He was alive but deeply unconscious. Williams nodded once to Cross.

The six of them then spent a moment pocketing their swimming gear and readying their weapons. Each of them was armed with a suppressor-equipped M4 carbine with a modified, shorter barrel for the inevitable close-quarters combat that this mission would require.

Brighton had complained about the weapon choice during the mission briefing, clearly hoping to use his prized AA-12 combat shotgun aboard the Black Anchor. However, Cross had accurately pointed out that the AA-12 just put too much lead into the air for this mission. And it was anything but precise — even if Brighton argued otherwise. Which he had. Repeatedly.

When everyone was ready, Cross gathered the squad and addressed them once more without words. He held up five fingers, reminding them of the number of hostile targets remaining onboard.

The Cubans' intelligence suggested that only six Hardwall mercenaries had gotten off their boat and subdued the oil platform's crew. Presumably, all five of the remaining mercs were armed and armored similarly to the sentry they'd just incapacitated. And they were sure to be in contact with each other via their headsets.

Cross tapped his watch, indicating it was only a matter of time before the other mercs noticed the missing man was no longer keeping in contact. That meant Shadow Squadron would have to move fast. And quietly.

According to the Cubans' intelligence, the Hardwall men were keeping the hostages near the helipad. Cross circled one finger in the air, mimicking a helicopter's spinning propeller. The message was clear: reaching the helipad was their first priority.

Walker knew this without having to read hand signals. Freeing the hostages was of the utmost importance on any mission. Engaging hostiles before securing the hostages almost always led to the loss of life.

Finally, Cross held up the think spherically signal one more time. As one, the men each gave a sharp nod. Together, they moved out along the catwalk to a set of stairs farther on.

As they moved, their eyes — and the muzzles of their carbines — kept in constant motion, scanning for trouble from all directions. Up, down, left, right — the enemies could come from anywhere.

The stairs up from the lower catwalk led up to the center of the structure. There they found a nexus of stairways, ladders, and walkways. It resembled a spider's nest made of metal. An array of dim LEDs created a creepy web of intersecting shadows and dark spaces where enemies could hide.

Walker strained his ears to listen for any sound of approaching mercenaries. He peered around, finding the stairs and walkways all labeled in Chinese. That wasn't a problem for him, since he was fluent, but he saw confusion on his teammates' faces, so Walker pointed out two separate paths that would take the team to the helipad.

Cross gave Walker a quick grateful nod and split the cell into two fireteams. He took Yamashita and Williams in one direction.

Walker led Brighton and Larssen in the other direction. He and his men crossed the underside of the helipad to a metal ladder on the far side. The three of them climbed until Walker reached the top and stopped. Carefully, he peered over the edge to take stock of the situation.

Twenty or so miserable-looking Chinese and Cuban hostages sat huddled in the center of the helipad. They were leaning against each other for warmth, or shivering with their arms wrapped around themselves. None of them spoke to each other or to their captors. To Walker's eyes, none of them appeared to be injured or otherwise suffering, but it would be Williams's job to say for sure.

Walker scanned for mercenaries. Two of them had been left to guard the hostages. Like the man down on the catwalk, the guards wore ballistic vests and carried submachine guns. One of them stood at the edge of the helipad looking out over the ocean, holding a writhing, pitiful Chinese crewman by his neck. The other guard stood by the group of hostages in the center. The second guard was laughing as the hostage in the mercenary's grasp squirmed.

"What's the matter?" the mercenary demanded of his terrified prisoner. "You don't have to use the bathroom anymore? Don't be shy, we're all guys here. Go ahead, do your business."

Walker clenched his teeth, struggling to repress the urge to aim his M4 one-handed and drop the thug where he stood. Yet, as satisfying as that might be, he couldn't be sure that the man wouldn't knock the prisoner overboard. And Walker didn't want to get into the habit of shooting people just because they were bullies.

The waterproof canalphone in Walker's right ear activated. Walker scanned across the helipad for Cross's fireteam. He could just make out Cross crouching at the top of the stairway leading onto the helipad on the other side of the platform.

Walker tapped his canalphone twice, returning Cross's signal. Cross took aim at the mercenary who was standing near the bulk of the hostages. Walker tensed on the ladder, preparing to move on the hostile who was harassing the captured crewman. He glanced back at Brighton, and held up three fingers. Then two. Then one . . .

The men launched into action, performing a variation on a set of maneuvers they had practiced many times in training. Cross stood up into full view of both guards and actually whistled to get their attention. It was just the kind of grandstanding that Walker found most annoying about Cross. However, it was undeniably effective: both guards turned to look at Cross in stunned surprise. That was when Walker mounted the helipad deck from the ladder.

Cross fired a single round. The guard folded up in the middle and sank to his knees. The hostages scrambled back away from him, parting for Cross as he rushed over to the downed mercenary.

A moment after Cross fired, the Hardwall mercenary by the edge of the helipad reacted with predictable cowardice. He yanked his gasping Chinese prisoner around in a half circle, clutching him from behind as a human shield. The mercenary brought his submachine gun up one-handed over the hostage's shoulder and pointed it at Cross.

Walker momentarily considered blasting the submachine gun out of the mercenary's hand. Instead, he aimed down at the mercenary's right thigh and fired. The bullet drilled right through his leg. The mercenary yelped and collapsed as his leg buckled, giving his human shield a chance to dash over to his huddled coworkers.

That's good at least, Walker thought. However, the wounded mercenary was aware of him now, and he was still perfectly capable of firing his weapon. As the merc flopped onto his back, he started to raise his gun with one hand.

"Drop it!" Walker demanded, reluctant to shoot an American citizen. "Now!"

Whether the man would have complied or not, Walker would never know. No sooner had Walker shouted his warning when Lieutenant Commander Cross raised his M4 and put the issue to rest, squeezing off a shot that caught the mercenary's MP5 right above the trigger. Hot metal shrapnel burst from the weapon as it flew out of the man's hand.

When the ruined submachine gun clattered to the deck, Cross shot it again. The weapon skittered over the side of the helipad and into the ocean.

Walker glanced at Cross, knowingly glaring at the man who'd potentially just saved his life. Cross flicked Walker a salute and a smirk.

Walker just shook his head and turned away. He wasn't going to begrudge Cross for taking the shot, but did the man have to show off when he did it?

Brighton and Larssen had climbed up onto the helipad behind Walker. They moved past him to zip-cuff the wounded mercenary. They pulled off his Bluetooth headset, bound his hands behind his back, and then treated his nonfatal leg wound.

Walker let the man lie and joined Cross. He was just finishing zip-cuffing the other mercenary. The Hardwall man lay on his stomach gasping for air, trying to recover from being struck by Cross's first shot. The bullet had been stopped by the ballistic vest, sparing his life, but knocking the wind out of him.

The hostages milled around, staring at the American soldiers with every imaginable variety of dumbfounded shock. Two incapacitated guards and no deaths. Walker had to admit that Cross did well. Really well.

Cross looked over at Walker and mouthed the word, "Clear?" Walker nodded. Williams came over at the same time, leaving Yamashita to keep a lookout for the rest of the hostiles. For the moment, none of the three remaining Hardwall mercs were anywhere to be seen. So Williams walked among the skittish hostages, looking for obvious signs of trauma and asking quiet questions.

Walker approached the hostage whom the second mercenary had tried to use as a human shield. "Are you hurt?" he whispered in Chinese.

The hostage's glassy, confused eyes slowly came back into focus. He shook his head. "They didn't hurt us," the man said in a soft, breathless voice.

"Do you know how many guards are left?" Walker asked.

"Four," the hostage answered. "One is on the catwalk below."

Walker nodded. That one was no longer a problem. "Where are the rest?" he asked.

"Operations control, with the station chief," the hostage said, pointing up toward the highest point of the facility. "They're talking to my government."

Walker relayed that information to Cross as Brighton and Larssen dragged the wounded mercenary over to them. The hostages backed off again. The mercenary moaned and tried to clutch at his leg with his zip-cuffed hands, cursing and yelling at them.

"Can we give this guy something to shut him up?" Brighton whispered in annoyance to Cross and Williams. "He's going to give our position away."

"I've got something for him," Cross said, stepping next to the wounded man. The mercenary looked up just as Cross slammed the butt of his carbine square into the merc's forehead. He lost consciousness instantly.

"Oh!" Brighton said, flinching and hiding his mouth behind his hand. Then, with a huge grin, he crouched over the unconscious mercenary. "You all right, man?" Brighton joked. "Walk it off, buddy."

"Shh!" Walker hissed, giving Brighton the noise-discipline signal. The combat controller snapped back to his feet, his grin not completely gone.

"All right, form up," Cross said softly, calling his men together. "We've got three hostiles remaining. They are in or around the operations center at the top of the facility." He addressed Williams. "Stay here and give the hostages a once-over." Then he looked at Larssen. "Watch his back, and keep an eye on the injured mercenaries."

"Sir," Williams and Larssen said together.

"You three are with me," Cross said to Walker, Yamashita, and Brighton. "Let's go sew this one up."

"Sir," Yamashita and Brighton said. Walker only gave a curt nod.

The fireteam joined Cross and left the helipad. With eyes and gun barrels sweeping back and forth and up and down, the men moved up a metal stairway to the platform's upper levels. The stairway wrapped around the outside of the platform and led into a narrow exterior walkway with pipes, valves, and gauges on both sides.

From there, the team passed through a wire-strewn computer center, a sparse recreation room with a television and ping-pong table, and the kitchen and dining area. Each room was messy and cluttered, evidence suggesting that the Hardwall men had rousted the crew in the middle of the workday. But there was no sign of more hostiles.

After clearing the rooms on that level, the team emerged onto another walkway. It wrapped around the other side of the structure, leading to another stairway to the topmost levels. Before the fireteam reached the stairs, Cross suddenly gave the stop signal. He looked over the rail at the helipad below. Walker looked down as well, trying to figure out what had caught the lieutenant commander's attention.

Walker saw that the hostages had grouped up at the edge of the helipad closest to the center of the platform. Williams moved among them, making sure everyone was in good health. Larssen was finishing zip-cuffing the two mercenaries to a stair railing. Faint smears of blood shone in the lights, indicating where Larssen had dragged the unconscious, wounded mercenary over to the rail.

"Lieutenants," Cross said, tapping his canalphone. "Did either of you call for medical evac?"

"Negative," Larssen and Williams answered, confusion evident in their voices.

Walker shared their confusion for a moment until he heard what Cross had already noticed: the sound of a helicopter chopping through the night air. The Navy had a Seahawk on standby in case of emergencies. But this helicopter wasn't coming from the right direction.

All too quickly, the aircraft roared up out of the darkness. It threw blinding halogen spotlights onto the helipad. One light played over the frightened hostages. The other spotlight illuminated Larssen, who was just crossing the helipad to rejoin Williams.

Cross and Walker both recognized the make of the helicopter as it rose into view. It was a Russian-made Mil Mi-8 — a troop transport and fast-attack gunship employed by both the Chinese and the Cuban militaries. The hostages' countrymen had come to rescue them at last. And now, in a huddled mass of terrified hostages, they had spotted an armed soldier standing over them.

The chopper turned its broadside toward the landing pad. A door in the side slid open. "Get out of there!" Walker and Cross called, hitting their canalphones simultaneously. Their warning was too late.

Machine guns flared to life as bullets drew a crisscrossing line across the concrete right toward Larssen. He had already started running away from the hostages and toward cover, but he wasn't fast enough. Larssen's body jerked, spun, and fell — all in the blink of an eye. He landed only a few yards short of safety.

The helicopter lowered toward the pad, preparing to offload soldiers. Cross pointed toward the helicopter. "Yamashita," he said through clenched teeth. "Tail rotor."

"Sir," Yamashita said without even a hint of emotion in his voice.

As one, Yamashita and Cross raised their weapons and fired in the helicopter's direction.

Walker had to admit his commanding officer was one of the best shots he had ever seen. Cross managed to squeeze off two three-round bursts that dug into the helicopter's hull just below the spinning main rotor. A third burst followed, raising a thick plume of white smoke. The helicopter's engine squealed like a wounded animal.

As good a shot as Cross was, however, Yamashita was even better. Firing one bullet at a time, he punched a line of holes in the helicopter's narrow tail, damaging the mechanism of the stabilizing rotor on the rear. The chopper bucked suddenly in the air and swerved wildly to one side. The pilot fought the spin and just barely managed to keep it from slamming into the edge of the helipad and crashing into the ocean below.

"Cease fire," Cross ordered. He and Yamashita lowered their weapons.

Walker saw the gunmen inside clinging to the handholds for dear life. They were unable to even find where the shots were coming from, much less return fire.

Barely able to control the aircraft, the pilot veered away from the Black Anchor and raced back the way he'd come. The helicopter fishtailed across the sky like a car swerving on an icy road.

Walker assumed the craft had launched from one of the vessels keeping watch on the water. He wondered if it would be able to make it back and land in one piece.

"Williams!" Cross barked, pointing over the rail toward where Larssen lay bleeding. It was technically a breach of operational protocol to refer to any of the team members by name while engaged in the field, but Walker could hardly fault the slip.

"Got him," came Williams's response over the canalphone. The corpsman rushed across the helipad and crouched over Larssen. He broke out the first-aid kit he hadn't yet needed for the hostages. A moment later, Williams said, "He's alive, Commander — barely. We need our evac chopper."

Cross had already produced a waterproof radio from one of his cargo pockets. He keyed in the emergency frequency. "Angel, this is Preacher," he called, mostly concealing the distress in his voice. "Man down. We need an airlift."

"Preacher, this is Angel," the pilot of the standby chopper called back. "Roger that, Preacher. ETA is five minutes."

Cross signed off. Then he tapped his canalphone and said, "Five minutes, Williams."

Williams sighed. "Sir."

"I'll gather our dive gear," Brighton said, turning as if to head back down below.

"Leave it," Cross said, stowing the radio. "You heard the man, we've only got five minutes."

"Sir?" Brighton said.

"Three hostiles left," Cross said, "and one hostage."

The distress from seeing Larssen down, and possibly dying, was absent from Cross's face now. In its place was a cold, grim anger. "Let's move," Cross barked.

"What about the SDV?" Brighton asked.

"The Navy can send a SEAL team if they want it back," Cross replied. "Now move out."

Brighton opened his mouth to say something else, but was silenced by the chattering of submachine gun fire. Bullets roared from ahead and above, ringing off the walls and the metal catwalk. Walker saw where the shots came from and realized what must have happened. The hostiles, unaware of Shadow Squadron's arrival, had heard the chopper open fire. The sudden departure of the helicopter had undoubtedly surprised them, but now they'd spotted Cross's fireteam, realizing they were still under siege. Fortunately, rather than move in for the kill or spread out to coordinate a crossfire, they'd simply opened fire from where they stood.

Two mercenaries were shooting from the catwalk one level up. Most of their shots were wild and panicked, though one glanced off Cross's helmet and another grazed Brighton across the shoulder blade.

The fireteam took cover. Walker had the clearest line of sight on the gunmen. He threw a line of fire up toward them, sending them diving backward for cover. Cross angrily signaled the team to move up and take the stairway, unwilling to let up on the mercenaries now that they'd engaged. Walker laid down cover fire to keep the mercenaries' heads down.

Hissing in pain from the wound on his back, Brighton rushed to a position at the foot of the steps and fired a few rounds up over the men's heads. Yamashita backtracked and scrambled up a ladder, looking for a level field of fire. One of the mercenaries saw him climbing and fired off what was left in his clip, but Walker drove him back with another stream of suppressing fire. The other mercenary fired back, forcing Yamashita to roll around a corner.

For a moment, no one moved and no one fired. The Hardwall men couldn't come down, and Yamashita had a firing line on their only avenue of escape. However, the mercs had clear lanes of fire on the only route the fireteam could take to reach them.

They were at a stalemate. Time was running out.

Suddenly, Lieutenant Commander Cross stood up. With his back to a wall, he moved toward a position directly beneath where the two mercenaries were holed up together. Then he signaled Walker to join Brighton at the base of the stairs and for the two of them to get ready to move.

Walker frowned. Yamashita wasn't in a position to provide covering fire. He only had a line on the mercenaries' escape route. If Brighton and Walker went up the stairs, the mercenaries would have a nice, narrow lane of fire to cut them down.

What is Cross thinking? Walker wondered.

Reading the expression on Walker's face, Cross winked, then gave him the think spherically sign. He reached into his

belt and drew an M84 flashbang grenade, then nodded at the walkway overhead.

Walker still wasn't sure exactly what Cross had in mind, but he got ready to move just the same. Cross pulled the pin but held the spoon and started counting down from five on his free hand. At two, he let go of the spoon but held onto the grenade, letting its fuse cook off in his hand. At zero, he signaled for Walker and Brighton to go, and the two men immediately rushed up the stairs together, staring down the long stretch of walkway between themselves and the mercs.

Hearing their approach, the mercs leaned around with their weapons. At the same moment, Cross took one step out from under the catwalk and threw his flashbang straight up in the air. It popped up over the rail right next to the mercenaries.

The flare and the concussion knocked the mercs off their feet, giving Walker and Brighton all the time they needed to close in and disarm them.

Cross and Yamashita quickly joined them. Walker signaled for Brighton to keep an eye out for the last mercenary. Then Walker went to work zip-cuffing the mercenaries to the catwalk.

With that done, Walker pulled out both men's Bluetooth headsets and put one to his left ear. Cross took the other one and did the same, signaling his fireteam to advance on the operations center.

"What the heck is going on out there?!" the last remaining mercenary shouted through the earpiece. "Answer me!"

"It's over," Cross said. "The rest of your men have been neutralized."

There was a long pause. Then a voice asked, "Who is this?" To Walker, the mercenary sounded scared and angry — a dangerous combination.

"Give yourself up," Cross responded. "You've run out of time, and I lack the patience to argue with you."

The mercenary let out a half-crazed cackle. "Oh, really?" he said. "Does that mean I should just kill my hostage, then?"

Cross frowned. Walker wondered if he had forgotten there was one hostage left.

The fireteam made it to the last walkway that led to the operations command station. The station had a large window on the side, but the lights inside went out as the team approached. Cross signaled a halt in front of the one door that led inside.

"No answer to that, huh?" the mercenary said. Walker could hear a second person whimpering in the background whenever the man talked. Walker glanced at Cross, but the commander remained silent.

"I'll tell you what," the merc said. "Me and my new friend here are going to get on my boat and leave, and you're going to let us. If anybody tries to 'neutralize' me, I swear —"

"Forget it," Cross snapped.

"No?" the merc said. "Then come in here and get me. The second I hear running footsteps, I'm putting two bullets in the back of this guy's head. Then I'm coming out with guns blazing."

Cross clenched his teeth. Then he closed his eyes and took a deep breath. He seemed to be considering daring the mercenary to do just that.

"Wait," Walker said, addressing both the mercenary and Cross. Walker held up a hand, silently urging Cross to give him a moment. Cross reluctantly nodded.

"Who's this now?" the mercenary demanded.

"Let me explain the situation to you," Walker said, his voice steady and heavy with authority. "In two minutes, a helicopter's coming to pick us up. And we're all going to be on it because you can be sure that the Cubans are already on their way here to clean up this mess their own way."

"Wait," the mercenary said, his voice sounding rattled suddenly. "Who are you guys? Are you Americans? Did Van Sant send you?"

"You're running out of time," Walker said. "If you don't come out, we're just going to leave and let you have this conversation with the Cubans. And I promise you, if you kill that hostage, you're on your own."

"Hang on a second, I —" the merc began.

"It's now or never," Walker said, interrupting him. Walker held up the earpiece so the merc could hear the approaching chopper. "Our ride's here. What's it going to be?"

At first, nothing happened. Then, slowly, the mercenary opened the operations center door and stepped out. He froze when he saw four M4 barrels pointing at him down the walkway.

"All right," the merc started to say. "Let's just —"

"Put your weapon down," Walker ordered him.

The mercenary dropped his MP5 on the ground and put his hands up. Uncertainty was written all over his face.

Cross dropped the Bluetooth headset and crunched it underfoot. He walked over to the mercenary.

"Kick the weapon over here," Walker said, coming up behind Cross. The mercenary slid the gun across the floor. Cross stepped over it, letting Walker catch it under one foot.

Williams's voice cut in on the team's canalphones. "Commander," the corpsman said, his voice somber. "Neil . . . is not going to make it."

Cross's face went dark.

"What?" the mercenary asked, unable to hear the conversation but reacting to the sudden change in Cross's expression. "What's going on?"

Cross brought up his M4 and smashed the butt stock across the bridge of the mercenary's nose. The mercenary stumbled backward, bounced off the operations center door and fell forward on his hands and knees. Cross placed his boot on the man's back, pressing him to the floor.

Walker came forward, planning to pull Cross back, but stopped when he saw the commander's rage had vanished. Without saying a word, Cross yanked the mercenary's arm up at an awkward angle and zip-cuffed it to the safety rail. Then he brushed past Walker, picked up the mercenary's MP5, and hurled it off the walkway. It clattered down through the superstructure and ended with a splash in the darkness.

"Move out!" Cross growled. He turned and walked back the way the fireteam had come, not bothering to check on the hostage in the operations center or the bound mercenary whimpering at his feet.

Yamashita fell into step behind Cross without a word. Brighton and Walker hesitated a moment, exchanging looks.

"Yikes," Brighton said.

Walker nodded. "Let's move," he said.

* * *

The Seahawk was halfway home. Since the team had left the Black Anchor, Cross had sat in silence, staring down at the shrouded, lifeless form resting on the deck below him. Second Lieutenant Neil Larssen had lived long enough to be brought onto the helicopter, but he'd died only a few minutes later. Walker had been trying without success to think of something to say to Cross that didn't sound forced. But no matter how hard he tried, he couldn't think of anything.

"We shouldn't have left them," Cross said. He looked up at Walker. "We should have brought all those Hardwall thugs back home with us to answer for what they did."

"That wasn't the mission," Walker said. "We had to do it this way so the Cubans could take credit for the rescue. Letting them save face is supposed to offset the damage Van Sant's people would've done to our country's reputation."

"But if we'd brought at least one back," Cross argued, "we could've had him give evidence against Van Sant and bring the whole organization down. But now all Van Sant has to do is claim they went rogue and condemn their actions. He'll probably get away with everything."

"He might try," Walker admitted. "But even if he pulls it off, I think Hardwall Security is about to find itself on some government lists that make it very hard to find good work."

"Maybe," Cross said. He sighed. "What a mess. This whole thing is going to be a diplomatic nightmare."

"Let the State Department worry about that," Walker said. "Just remember that for your part, you did everything right."

"Not everything," Cross said quietly. His eyes went back to the body at his feet.

"That wasn't your fault," Walker said.

"'*The lives of my teammates and the success of our mission depend on me,*'" Cross said, quoting from the US Navy SEAL creed.

"'*In the worst of conditions,*'" Walker said, quoting a different section, "'*the legacy of my teammates steadies my resolve and silently guides my every deed.*'"

"'*I will draw on every remaining ounce of strength to protect my teammates,*'" Cross countered. "I didn't protect him, did I?"

"Knowing full well the hazards of my profession, I will always strive to uphold the prestige, honor, and esprit de corps of my regiment," Walker said.

Cross raised an eyebrow. "What's that from?" he asked.

"The Ranger creed," Walker said. "I'm not sure that's exactly how it goes, but that's the general idea behind it. Neil was a Ranger . . . wouldn't you say he lived up to that standard?"

"Always," Cross said.

"Then mourn him, and honor him," Walker said. "But don't make his loss about yourself. If you start down that road, you'll end up feeling guilty whenever you look around and don't see him. Trust me: I've been right where you are now."

Cross was quiet for a long while, apparently considering the chief's words. But bit by bit, Cross seemed to relax a little. He looked up. "Does that mean we actually have a second thing in common with each other, Chief Walker?" he asked.

"Something else?" Walker asked. "What was the first thing?"

"The fact that we're both SEALs, of course," Cross said.

Walker smirked.

"Well, don't get ahead of yourself, Commander," Walker deadpanned. "I'm an SDV SEAL, after all . . ."

Cross grinned. "Right, Chief." He took a slow, deep breath. "And thanks."

Walker nodded. "Sir."

MISSION DEBRIEFING

OPERATION

BLACK ANCHOR 1234

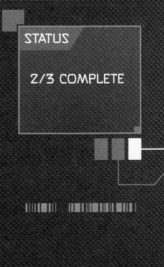

MISSION COMPLETE

PRIMARY OBJECTIVE

- Secure the oil rig platform and transport hostages to safety

STATUS

2/3 COMPLETE

SECONDARY OBJECTIVES

- Minimize damage done to Hardwall mercenaries

x Avoid contact with the Cuban and Chinese forces

3245.98

WALKER, ALONSO

RANK: Chief Petty Officer
BRANCH: Navy SEAL
PSYCH PROFILE: Walker is Shadow Squadron's second-in-command. His combat experience, skepticism, and distrustful nature make him a good counter-balance to Cross's command.

I had to reprimand the other members of Shadow Sqadron for neglecting to file their *Black Anchor* debriefings in a timely manner. But overall, they performed admirably in the field. All the hostages were recovered unharmed, and the men kept their emotions under control even when one of our own was shot down. Cross was really shaken up over losing Larssen. We all were. But we were able to keep it together and complete the mission.

Second Lieutenant Neil Larssen was a good man and a good soldier. He will be missed.

— Chief Petty Officer Alonso Walker

ERROR

UNAUTHORIZED

USER MUST HAVE LEVEL 12 CLEARANCE
OR HIGHER IN ORDER TO GAIN ACCESS
TO FURTHER MISSION INFORMATION.

2019.581

LOADING MISSION:

EAGLE DOWN

$2145.98 ● ● ●

1216.062

2012.241

CLASSIFIED

MISSION BRIEFING

EAGLE DOWN 1234

This one's going to be a solo mission for little ol' me. I'll be running a joint-government effort to shut down the Colombian drug network, or nexus, that is mainlining illegal drugs into the veins of the US. My target is a shipyard along the Pacific coast in the Colombian jungle. Local Colombian soldiers will help me assess the site. After that, I'll call in an air strike to shut down the nexus for good.

The rest of Shadow Squadron just have to launch the strike, then pick me up once I finish doing my thing.

– Staff Sergeant Edgar Brighton

3245.98 ● ● ●

COLOMBIA

PRIMARY OBJECTIVES

- Covert insertion via parachute

- Rendezvouz with Colombian task force

- Locate shipyard

- Call in coordinates for precision air strike

SECONDARY OBJECTIVES

- Minimize casualties

- Foster positive relations with the Colombian task force

- Remain undetected

1932.788

0412.981

1624.054

EAGLE DOWN

Right up until the moment he touched ground in the jungle, Brighton's assessment of the mission was that *Operation: Nexus* was going just fine. In fact, Brighton thought it was a nice change of pace to be doing something on his own — and on solid ground — after the last two seaborne, team-based ops.

This mission was a joint US and Colombian venture aimed at striking a powerful blow to the illegal Colombian drug network, or nexus. Their primary target was a low-tech shipyard hidden somewhere in the roadless jungles along Colombia's Pacific coast.

Somewhere among looping rivers and mangrove trees was a facility that produced vessels capable of smuggling up to ten tons of cocaine at a time. And they were virtually undetectable. These vehicles, nicknamed "narco-subs," were small fiberglass crafts capable of running just below the ocean's surface, guided by periscope and GPS. A small crew could take one of these boats from the shipyard, sneak down the riverways to the coast, and get to the ocean with ease. From there, the narco-subs headed north to the coast of Mexico. Then they docked in various concealed ports to offload their illegal drugs to waiting distributors.

In recent years, this system caused a sharp rise in cocaine coming from Colombia, into Mexico, then into the United States. The Mexican Sinaloa drug cartel cut, distributed, and sold the cocaine. Elements of the *Fuerzas Armadas Revolucionarias de Colombia* (or FARC) rebel guerilla army produced the cocaine. FARC also outfitted the narco-subs and recruited the terrified fishermen who piloted them.

When the Sinaloa cartel sold the cocaine abroad, it gave back a percentage of the profits to the FARC guerillas. The guerillas then used the money to buy weapons, equipment, and supplies for their ongoing attempts to overthrow the rightful government of Colombia.

After a lot of talking about the problem and a lot of planning what to do about it, the US and Colombia had decided on a strategy that would cripple the FARC/Sinaloa drug trafficking arrangement. The Colombians had some general information about where they believed the narco-sub shipyard was hidden. However, they had lost every soldier and police officer they'd sent into the jungle. Even worse, none of them were able to confirm the shipyard's suspected location.

The Colombians claimed they were committed to assaulting and shutting down the hidden shipyard. However, they needed help from the Americans to actually find the base and gather solid intel about it. They didn't want a large number of American troops and military machinery plunging into their backyard to fight their battles for them. Instead, they just wanted some help getting off the ground.

That help came in the form of Staff Sergeant Edgar Brighton, the team's combat controller. Because of his unique set of skills, and fluency in Spanish, Brighton was chosen by Lieutenant Commander Cross for the role.

The Colombians welcomed Shadow Squadron to use the tiny military base on the otherwise uninhabited Malpelo Island. Then the Colombians set up their own joint military and police task force to coordinate with the Americans. They'd all been working and training together for a few weeks and were now ready to put *Operation: Nexus* into motion.

The first stage was to improve the Colombians' intelligence about the shipyard before an air raid kicked off the final stage. Brighton's job was to head out alone into hostile territory and perform special reconnaissance. He would then report his findings back to Cross at their makeshift headquarters. In the field, it was his job to maintain contact with whatever aerial units were available. That meant Brighton had to organize fast-attack fighters, heavy bombers, and emergency air transportation. He had to keep them on task, on target, and out of each other's way.

Brighton was also responsible for direct action. He stood side by side with his fellow soldiers when they engaged the enemy. Plenty of air support was on hand for *Operation: Nexus*, so it was up to Brighton to get in first. It was up to him to make everything ready for the rest of his team. But he would not be alone.

To help him in this task, he was ordered to link up in the jungle with an advance team of Colombians from the military and police task force. They would point him in the right direction once he got his boots on the ground. Then they would watch his back while he gathered intelligence and reported back to Cross and the rest of Shadow Squadron.

The ride by boat and then car from Malpelo Island to the forward staging base in Popayan had been pleasant enough. It gave Brighton a chance to shoot the breeze with his commanding officer. He also got to chat with the Colombian soldiers who'd come to retrieve him. Being members of an elite group of covert special operatives, Cross and Brighton couldn't say anything personal about themselves or their service records to the Colombians. But the local policemen and soldiers in the task force seemed to love small talk.

The pre-mission briefing between Brighton, Cross, and Major Timoleon Gaitan (the leader of the task force), had gone well. However, Brighton could tell the Colombian major was nervous about how young Brighton was. Gaitan had kept his opinion to himself, though, so Brighton hadn't been forced to list the number of specialized training schools whose programs he'd aced after Combat Control School. He knew he'd been selected for the Shadow Squadron at such a young age for very good reasons. But Major Gaitan didn't ask what those reasons were. That was probably for the best, though, as Brighton didn't want to embarrass his host.

The flight out over the jungle was just like the dozens of others Brighton had participated in all over the world. The passenger compartment of the Cessna 206 that the Colombian Police provided for transport was a little cramped. Or, at least it felt that way with the air crew, the jumpmaster, and Brighton's load of gear all jammed together.

Sadly, Brighton didn't have the time to chat with Popayan's team due to last-minute checks of his gear and parachute rigging. However, a few jokes and his pleasant manner seemed to set everyone at ease. That is, as at ease as men can be in a cramped, dark airplane cabin over hostile territory in the early morning hours. But if anyone could pull it off, Brighton figured he was the man. He loved meeting new people and enjoyed nothing more than making new friends.

The pilot said over the intercom that the plane was over the jump zone. Brighton donned his night-vision mask, then stepped up to the Cessna's side door beside the jumpmaster. With the mask's several 16mm intensifier tubes sticking out around his eyes, it gave Brighton an eerie, insect-like appearance. In fact, Brighton saw the jumpmaster do a double-take as he approached. Strange looks aside, Brighton preferred the expanded view range of his panoramic mask to the ones the rest of Shadow Squadron used. The other models made Brighton feel like his field of vision was limited.

Following the jumpmaster's pointed finger, Brighton located a tiny clearing a few hundred yards from the bank of the muddy river below. From its center, a small infrared beacon blinked. That was the signal the Colombians' advance team had set up to guide Brighton to them.

It was visible only via night-vision equipment from above, thankfully. Brighton didn't want to land amidst a team of armed hostiles.

Clearing his thoughts, Brighton readied himself to jump. From this height, it was going to be tricky hitting the bull's-eye on the clearing, but he wasn't worried. A pre-dawn precision jump into heavy jungle was nothing compared to having to deal with drug-dealing guerillas shooting at you. So, with a well-trained and fully confident mind, he awaited the signal.

"Go!" the jumpmaster yelled. A moment later, Brighton hurled himself out the door and into the darkness. The elation of his first few seconds of free-fall made Brighton's head swim. Skydiving had always thrilled him, ever since his first tandem jump with his father at age fifteen. He loved to let the thrill of the descent fill his mind as the earth soared up toward him. But this time, he allowed himself only a few fleeting moments of joy before he let his training take over.

Brighton spread his arms and legs to right himself in the air and maximize wind resistance. Then he checked the altimeter and GPS device mounted on his wrist. Finally he shifted in the air until he located the target beacon with his goggles once more.

The easy, gradual turn gave him a good opportunity to observe the lay of the land. With his eyes, he traced the many river inlets and outlets, memorizing the few landmarks he could make out with his night-vision mask. When he was low enough, he opened his chute.

Brighton bent himself into a wide downward spiral. He was confident that would put him within ten yards of the clearing, if not dead center. Easily, in fact. The tricky part, however, was the actual landing. All of Brighton's gear made him heavy under the chute.

As expected, Brighton managed to hole-in-one the small clearing. But when he hit the muddy ground, the extra weight made him stumble. A gust of wind pushed his chute into the branches overhead. Brighton was forced to leave it dangling for a moment to set down his secondary pack and squirm out of his rigging. Standard procedure was to bury his jump gear after landing in order to minimize the chances that enemy forces would discover his intrusion. He had just opened his pack to grab his shovel when he heard several pairs of boots squelching through the mud.

Brighton saw a group of eight men in old-school camouflage uniforms emerge from the jungle shadows. They were ragged, hard-looking men. To Brighton, they looked more like hardened special forces troops than policemen. And they all looked like they were quite a bit older than Brighton, though that could just be due to the wear and tear of years of combat experience.

"Hey, fellas," Brighton greeted them in Spanish. "Could you have picked a smaller clearing for my landing? I could almost see this one from the sky."

"You're the one Gaitan sent?" the one closest to Brighton asked. He had the gravelly voice of a lifetime smoker.

Brighton nodded. The man said nothing, but instead signaled to another soldier behind Brighton's back.

"Give me a sec to set up my radio," Brighton said. "If one of you could pull that chute down and bury it for me, I'd appreciate it."

Brighton knelt beside his pack. He'd just opened the waterproof flap and turned up the whip antenna when a man came up behind him. Without thinking, Brighton handed the folded-up shovel over his shoulder.

"Here you go," Brighton said. "I appreciate the help —"

Fifty thousand volts of electricity surged into Brighton from between his shoulder blades. Every nerve and muscle in his body blazed with pain. Brighton collapsed in a heap. He felt like he had no control over his own body.

He had endured this exact sensation before during his training. Otherwise, he wouldn't even have known what had just happened. But in the back of his mind, far from the pain, Brighton understood he'd been zapped with a stun gun.

No sooner had Brighton come to this realization than he received another jolt. Brighton tried to yell, but his mouth wouldn't open. His teeth were clenched shut due to the muscles spasming through his entire body. While Brighton lay gasping, one of the Colombians turned him over onto his back. The rest of the soldiers gathered around to look at him. One of them held the flashing IR beacon in his hand. At this close range, its intense glare stung Brighton's eyes through his night-vision mask.

A man knelt in front of him. He held the stun gun up where Brighton could see it. "He's still conscious," the man said, sneering. He lowered the stun gun toward Brighton again.

It's not a knockout wand, man, Brighton thought. But he was in too much pain to move, let alone speak. Fortunately, one of the other soldiers grabbed the stun gun out of the man's hand before he could zap Brighton again.

"Stop playing around," a voice said. Brighton glanced up to see the butt of an M16 assault rifle just as it came down hard on his night-vision mask. Brighton saw stars and heard the sickening sound of shattering glass at once.

Then he fell into total darkness.

* * *

When Brighton finally regained consciousness, he had no idea how long he'd been out. It could have been hours. Or even days. It probably wasn't days, but Brighton had no way of knowing.

The only thing Brighton knew for sure was that his head felt like it had been split open. A heavy, blinding throb emanating from above his right eye pounded in time with his pulse.

That would be where the Colombian smashed me in the face with the butt of that M16, he realized.

As his senses returned, Brighton scanned the area to take stock of his situation. Turning his head gingerly on his stiff neck, he saw that he was inside a large ten-by-ten room on top of a concrete slab. It had a corrugated metal roof and walls.

The air was filled with jungle humidity, and the room lacked any sort of ventilation. What the room did have was bright lights on the ceiling and on the wall in front of him. They shined right in his face. Brighton could also hear a generator rumbling behind one of the walls. He tried to raise a hand to shield his aching eyes from the glare. But when his hand didn't move, he realized his wrists had been handcuffed to the chair he was sitting in.

The old dentist chair was upholstered in cracked, faded vinyl. As he glanced down at his ankles, he noticed they were cuffed to the footrest sticking out in front of him. His boots and socks were gone.

"FARC," Brighton grumbled.

There was no question he'd been captured by the very same FARC rebels that Shadow Squadron and the Colombian government were working together to bring down. The only real question was what the guerillas who'd captured him had done to the real joint military and police task force. They were supposed to meet Brighton at the drop point. The fact that the FARC guerillas had been waiting around the IR beacon for Brighton implied that much. And the fact that they'd mentioned Major Gaitan by name proved that Brighton's capture hadn't been a result of dumb bad luck.

Brighton figured that someone on the advance team was a traitor. That person could have easily warned the rebels about *Operation: Nexus*. But the sinister feel of the room in which Brighton found himself suggested that FARC had probably used torture to extract the information.

And Brighton fully expected that he would be next. As if on cue, Brighton heard a door open behind him. A Colombian man slowly walked around him into view. He wore clean olive-drab fatigues, rubber gloves, and a baby-blue surgical mask. Only his eyes were visible beneath the brim of his hat. He was writing a note in a small, spiral-bound notepad when he noticed that Brighton was awake. The man tucked his pad and a pen into his hip pocket and checked Brighton's pulse. Then he prodded gingerly at the lump over Brighton's right eye. Brighton eyed him warily through his examination. The man said nothing.

"Can I get some water?" Brighton asked.

The Colombian still said nothing. "Maybe a sandwich? I'd name some names for a Philly cheese steak right about now."

The Colombian stood up, then walked behind Brighton toward the entrance without a word.

"And get me some aspirin when you come back," Brighton called out. "My head is killing me."

The door opened behind Brighton, then quickly closed. "All right, take your time," Brighton said. "Think about it."

Another ten minutes or so went by. Then the door opened and several sets of feet shuffled inside. Nobody came around into Brighton's field of view at first, but he heard them moving around behind him. Someone kept making trips in and out. The person's breathing was strained by carrying something heavy.

It took a couple of repetitions before Brighton figured out what it was. Someone was carrying in heavy plastic carboys full of water, like the ones that plugged into the top of office watercoolers. By Brighton's count, they brought in a total of six containers. When that was done, someone dragged in a rolling cart then shut the door. Only then did the visitors finally come into Brighton's line of sight.

On his right came the same Colombian who Brighton had seen before. Now the gloves and mask were gone, but the pen and pad were still in his pocket. He wore a stethoscope around his neck and held an ophthalmoscope in his hand. The man leaned over Brighton and used the opthalmoscope to peer into his eyes. Then he checked Brighton's heartbeat and breathing with the stethoscope. Not once did the man's eyes meet Brighton's.

Behind the "doctor" stood two more Colombians wearing camo fatigues. Brighton recognized them from the clearing in the jungle. One of them was the guy who'd zapped him with the stun gun. The other was the one who'd knocked him out with the rifle.

"Hey, man," Brighton said to the man examining him. "Where's my aspirin?"

Someone else came up on Brighton's left. "Good morning," the voice chirped.

Brighton was quite surprised by the voice. For one thing, the speaker used English with a Spanish accent. Brighton wasn't all that great with languages, but he was pretty sure the speaker was Mexican, not Colombian. That almost certainly meant she was on loan to the FARC guerillas from the Sinaloa drug cartel in Mexico.

More good news, Brighton thought sarcastically. *That means she's experienced — and a hired professional.*

Yet Brighton was more surprised that the speaker was a woman. As she stepped into view, Brighton saw that she appeared to be in her mid-thirties and in excellent physical shape.

"My name is Morgan Saenz," the woman said. "I represent the Sinaloa cartel."

Brighton grimaced. *I hate being right all the time,* he thought.

The woman pushed a steel tray on a rolling metal cart up to the side of Brighton's chair, then stood next to it. A white hotel-style hand towel covered a handful of mysterious lumps on the tray. Her fingers danced over them while she looked Brighton right in the eyes.

"It doesn't concern me that you know my name, young man," Saenz said. "Let that explain to you the situation you are in. It doesn't matter how much information you learn about me or our operation here. That is because you'll never have an opportunity to reveal it to anyone."

"Why's that?" Brighton asked despite knowing the answer perfectly well.

"Because we're going to kill you," Saenz said flatly. "Only the circumstances of your death are up to you. If you answer my questions freely and in detail, I'll see to it that you drift off to peaceful sleep and never wake up. If you resist me at first but eventually break down and cooperate, I'll reward you with a large-caliber bullet through the head. An equally quick death, if not so peaceful."

Saenz paused a moment for effect and stood in front of Brighton's chair. The harsh lights on the wall behind her cast her face in shadow. It made a halo of light shine through her long, black, shining hair. Brighton had to admit that it was an intimidating sight.

"But listen carefully, though, to what will happen if you test my patience," Saenz told him. She leaned over and gripped the arms of Brighton's chair. She put her face right in front of his. "I fully expect you to resist at first. I wouldn't respect you if you didn't. But if you keep it up too long, I will punish you. If you still refuse to cooperate, your punishment will get worse. Eventually, there will come a point when I'm no longer interested in your cooperation."

Saenz stood back, then paused. She placed her hands on her hips, and said, "When that happens, I'm going to see to it that you die in more pain than you can possibly imagine. Nothing you say or do can save you at that point. Even if you try to cooperate, I won't change my mind. Do you understand?"

"You're making yourself pretty clear," Brighton said quietly.

"Good," Saenz said. She slowly stood. "Now, this will be your best opportunity to start talking. Do you have anything to say?"

"Yeah, actually," Brighton replied. "For an evil person, you're pretty hot."

Saenz shook her head in disappointment. "Oh well," she said with a sigh. "It was your opportunity to waste."

Brighton gave his best attempt at a shrug. "I got to be me," he said with a grin.

Saenz looked over to the doctor and the two FARC guerillas behind Brighton. At a nod from her, the doctor pulled down the back of Brighton's chair. Brighton now lay on his back staring up at the harsh lights on the ceiling. He struggled against his restraints and tried to pull himself back upright, but he couldn't move. He could only watch helplessly as the camouflage-clad guerillas shifted behind him.

Saenz lifted the hand towel from her tray and handed it to the doctor, who came around to the top of Brighton's chair. The doctor wrapped the towel around Brighton's face. He fastened the towel in place and stepped back. The guerillas moved forward.

When Brighton heard the sound of sloshing water, he realized what was about to happen. He took a deep breath. A second later, the guerillas popped the valve in the top of the plastic carboy they carried between them and upended the whole jug over Brighton's head.

The water was shockingly cold. It immediately soaked the towel over Brighton's face, turning it into an icy hand clamping down over his mouth and nose.

The water came down and down and down, threatening to go on longer than Brighton could hold his breath. It ran up his nose and would have made him panic if he hadn't been expecting it. Fortunately, the water in the carboy ran out before he had to breathe again. His lungs burned, but he made it through the first torrent without freaking out and filling his lungs with water.

"Are you new at this, or something?" Brighton asked, spitting out water and trying not to gasp. "You're supposed to ask me some questions before you waterboard me."

"That was just a demonstration," Saenz said as she picked something up off the metal tray beside the chair. "I want you to understand that we're not opposed to hurting you."

"I'll remember that if you ever do hurt me," Brighton joked. That comment got a chuckle out of Saenz, which Brighton considered a small victory.

"Our purpose is to gather information," Saenz said. "The soldier we brought here before you — the one you were supposed to meet, in fact — was not very helpful to us before he died."

"I wondered how you guys got the drop on me so fast," Brighton said. Behind him, he heard the guerillas picking up and opening another water carboy. Still flat on his back, Brighton listened for sound cues that they were about to dump it on him so that he'd know when to hold his breath.

"You know I'm not going to talk, though, right?" Brighton said.

"Not at first," Saenz said. "But do remember what I said about resistance. A stubborn waste of my time will be punished severely. So, let's start simply with some control questions. What is your name, what branch of the American military do you represent, and what is your rank?"

Brighton took a moment to collect his thoughts and prepare himself for what was coming. In his torture-resistance training, his instructor had taught him to think of something he loved that made him happy. By holding onto that thought, the pain was easier to manage. For Brighton, that thought was the superhero comic books he read every chance he got.

Brighton grinned. "My name is Bruce Banner," he said. "And you're starting to make me angry. You wouldn't like me when I'm angry."

Saenz frowned. She gestured to the men behind Brighton. Instantly, a gallon of water came down on him. Thankfully he heard the carboy slosh, so he was able to get a small breath in before any water hit him. He expected it to go on like it had before, but it stopped suddenly and the guerillas backed off.

Brighton expected the question to be repeated, but Saenz had another idea. She hit the trigger on a stun gun and let the electricity sizzle for a second so Brighton could identify the sound.

He didn't even have time to struggle before Saenz turned the crackling weapon on him, touching his left thigh just above the knee. She only did it for a second, but it was more than enough.

The second she stopped, the guerillas poured out water again. This time, Brighton had no way to hold his breath. Wracked with pain by the stun gun, his body instinctively tried to breathe. He sucked in water instead. His body immediately switched to panic mode. His mind began to scream that he was drowning, drowning, drowning!

It was all Brighton could do to force himself not to breathe in or out. He just locked his chest muscles and willed himself not to cough, not to gag, not to cry out. He forced himself just to hold on and ride out the pain as best he could. Fortunately the second rush of water stopped as quickly as the first one had. He held his breath another couple of seconds just to be sure, then sucked in an icy, wet lungful of water that made him cough and choke.

"Perhaps you misunderstood the question," Saenz said. Brighton's heart was beating so loudly in his ears that he could barely hear her. "What is your name, what branch of the military do you represent, and what is your rank?"

"Okay, okay, I'll tell you!" Brighton said between coughs, sounding as serious as possible. "I do work for the United States government. In fact, I'm part of a secret team called The Avengers. My real name is Steve Rogers . . ." Brighton stopped for a moment to catch his breath. ". . . But the world knows me as Captain America."

Another jolt of electricity hit Brighton, cutting him off. It was longer this time. Then more water. Brighton fought his panic instincts as best he could, but his head had tilted back from the shock, and the water hit him right in the nose. For a while, it felt like he was trapped under the ocean waves. He coughed so hard that white lightning bolts crisscrossed behind his closed eyelids.

Then, somehow, it was over and he could breathe again — but just barely.

"Your name, your branch, your rank," Saenz said, matter-of-factly. "These aren't even the difficult questions."

"My name . . ." Brighton croaked, ". . . is Batman."

* * *

After several more rounds of questioning, Brighton had lost the ability to mark the passing of time. It seemed to go on for hours. Half a day, at least. Maybe longer. The constancy of the lighting and the minimal variation in temperature blurred everything into a meaningless haze as his tormentor worked him over.

Throughout the ordeal, Brighton convinced himself that he was winning a small victory through sheer stubbornness. A session like this, he knew, was all about the balance of power between torturer and victim, and he was determined to hold on to whatever scrap of power he could. If he was able to resist giving information to the enemy, great. But if he could actively annoy the enemy with comic book references in the process, he was at least playing the game by his own rules.

The Air Force's SERE (Survival, Escape, Resistance, Evasion) training after Combat Control School had helped prepare Brighton somewhat for this kind of situation. Part of the training dealt with how to steel yourself against the rigors of torture, like holding on to your favorite memories. But there were no secret techniques to magically make someone immune to pain, fear, or exhaustion. No, the largest part of resistance training had been more about describing common forms of torture and demonstrating what sensations those techniques inflicted on the human body.

Removing the element of the unknown from the equation made the idea of torture less intimidating. The instructors could then work with students one-on-one to try to help them find the individual emotional strength within that would help them survive against the enemy in the darkest of times.

That said, there was a marked difference between being taught what to expect from an "enhanced interrogation" and actually being subjected to torture. One of the lessons Brighton remembered most clearly from his very first day of SERE training was his grizzled, leathery instructor telling the class that torture breaks everyone eventually. There was only so much the body could take before the mind collapsed. Even Captain America himself would eventually turn into a willing collaborator.

No, the best a captured soldier could do was to keep his eyes and ears open for the means to escape when it presented itself. Brighton had already taken a step toward that goal, but the means were worthless without the opportunity. That meant that he had to endure whatever Saenz and her lackeys dished out until they got frustrated enough to leave him alone for a while.

So, Brighton dug deep and refused to give in to the fear and desperation that welled up whenever Saenz's stun gun jolted him and the water came rushing down. He let himself cough and choke and hack, but he just kept telling himself that no matter how bad it got, it was too early for Saenz to really, truly want him dead. As far as she knew, he had information she valued. He didn't believe she was ready to let him die, so he had no fear — well, a diminished fear — of what she would do to him.

At some point during that first session, Saenz slowed down. Brighton could tell that his stubborn behavior was getting to her. After the fifteenth time asking him the same question about who he was, then getting superhero names in response, she changed tactics. Now she asked broader questions. How many Americans were working with the Colombians on *Operation: Nexus*? How long had they been ordered to stay in Colombia? What did they know about the specifics of the Sinaloa-FARC smuggling operation? Who was Brighton's commanding officer? Saenz gave Brighton a long pause after asking each question, then signaled to her goons when he disappointed her.

During that phase of the interrogation, she gave Brighton a basic outline of the areas of concern the leadership of the Sinaloa-FARC operation had about the American presence. It felt like a minor victory to Brighton — that he was getting far more information from his own torturer than she was able to get from him. But as that phase neared its conclusion — and the water in the carboys ran low — Brighton realized he was weakening. He didn't feel any nearer to collaborating than he had been before, but his body was worn out from all the abuse. He let three questions go by without being able to come up with a comics reference in place of an honest answer. It had come to the point where Saenz was punishing him for silence rather than willful disobedience. At last, the tone of her voice suggested that she realized they'd hit a wall.

"I suppose you'll be glad to know we're finished for now," Saenz said.

The doctor in olive drab peeled back the sodden hand towel from Brighton's face and leaned over him to check his vitals again.

"I probably should have given you a break some time ago," Saenz said, "but I was impressed by your extensive comic book knowledge. You and I, it seems, have surprisingly similar taste in reading."

"Cool," Brighton tried to say, through his throat was too raw to speak very loudly. "So you wanna go get a bite to eat together?"

"I'll pass," Saenz said. "Another reason we stayed so long today is that I wanted to convince myself whether this method of questioning was likely to have any effect on you in the long term. You might be proud to hear that it doesn't seem very effective. Therefore, when next we meet, I'll be upgrading the punishments you earn."

"Maybe next time you could try some positive reinforcement," Brighton said, his voice mockingly helpful.

"Maybe bring me an ice cream cake or nice rib-eye steak. You know, I haven't seen the new Batman movie yet . . ."

"I have something else in mind," Saenz said. "Allow me to demonstrate."

She picked up something from the steel tray beside Brighton and flicked her wrist like she was cracking a whip. He recognized the distinctive sound the object made. Saenz had just whipped open a collapsible baton.

"That doesn't sound like ice cream cake," Brighton said.

Saenz said nothing. With a cold, grim expression, she walked past the end of the chair and raised the baton for a backhand swing. Brighton began to say something to change her mind, but she quickly struck him across the soles of both bare feet. Saenz didn't put much power into the blow, but that didn't matter. Brighton howled as pain exploded up his legs.

Saenz collapsed the baton. Carefully, she placed it back on the tray. Brighton did his best to remain silent, but he couldn't stop his body from shaking due to the pain. "Something for you to think about while I'm gone," Saenz said. Her voice was thick with self-satisfaction at Brighton's obvious suffering. "That's how I'll be punishing you for unhelpful answers during our next session. From now on, every session you force me to put you through will be worse than the one before."

She leaned back over Brighton, then pulled the back of his chair upright so that he was sitting up again. Her voice dropped to a secret whisper. "Thus far, I'm neither bored nor impressed with you, young man," she said. "Most soldiers your age can make it through at least two sessions with me with their dignity still intact. Any more than that, though . . . and you'll get to see what I look like when *I* am the one who is angry. And believe me, you would not like me when I am angry."

And with that, Morgan left the room.

Alone now, Brighton's beaten-down body could have done with some quality rest. Unfortunately, sleep was out of the question. For one thing, it was too hot to sleep. The blazing sun over the humid South American jungle turned the metal-and-concrete room into a stifling oven. Also, the lights glared down on him from every angle, which would've been far from restful even in peaceful circumstances. He might as well have been staring at the sun.

Of course, that was his torturer's intention. Bright lights and uncomfortable temperatures kept a man from sleeping, and sleep deprivation contributed to the collapse of a man's judgment and willpower. That was torture in and of itself.

Brighton couldn't allow himself to sleep now, anyway. He had no idea how long it would be before Saenz and her goons came back. The last thing he wanted was to let them catch him in the act of what he was about to do. He imagined they'd only be rougher on him if they discovered he was trying to escape.

As for the means of his escape, Brighton had secured it the moment Saenz introduced herself. When the FARC guerilla doctor leaned over Brighton with the ophthalmoscope to look in his eyes, Brighton slipped the retractable ballpoint pen out of the man's hip pocket. He then pushed it down into the padding on the arm of his chair through a crack in the ancient vinyl that covered it.

During his interrogation, Brighton had kept his forearm over the rip and the bulge the pen made. No matter how much it hurt, he hadn't shifted its position. Otherwise, his captors would have spotted it. Now that he was alone, Brighton worked the pen back out of its hiding place. To Brighton's red and weary eyes, the cheap piece of plastic junk looked like a treasure made of gold for one simple reason: it had a flat, detachable metal clip.

Carefully, to ensure he didn't drop the pen, Brighton slid his fingernail underneath the clip and bent it backward until it stood out from the body of the pen at a right angle. Then he turned the pen upside down in his hand. Barely breathing, he inserted the end of the clip into the keyhole of the handcuff holding his right hand. When it was firmly in place, he used the pen for leverage and bent the end of the clip into a right angle. Brighton pulled the clip out and turned the pen around in his hand. Then he reinserted the bent clip and bent another right angle into it going the opposite way.

Despite the urgency of what he was doing, Brighton worked slowly and steadily as if he had all the time in the world. As tired as he was, he knew that if he rushed, he would most certainly screw it up. Then when Saenz returned and she figured out what Brighton had been doing, he'd have the devil to pay.

When the work of bending the pen's clip into a crude

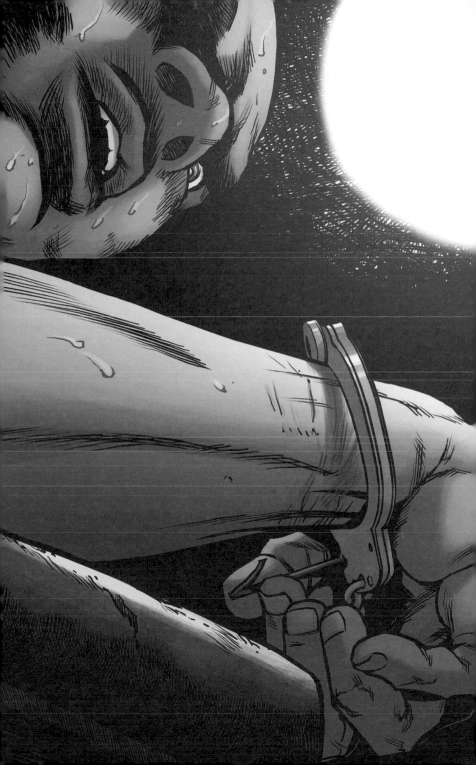

lock-pick shim was done, Brighton paused for a second to calm back down and steady his hands.

Now came the moment of truth. Gritting his teeth and breathing steadily, he worked his shim into the handcuff's lock. Patiently, slowly, he twisted the pen and applied pressure on the lock mechanism inside. Millimeter by millimeter, he twisted, twisted, and twisted . . .

Brighton bit back a howl of triumph as the lock disengaged and the handcuff swung open. Sparing no time to celebrate, he unlocked the cuff from the chair, then began picking the lock on the cuff around his other hand. It took all of Brighton's focus to remain calm as he deftly opened it, freeing his other hand.

But he wasn't free yet — both of his feet were still bound. Slowly, calmly, Brighton bent his stiff back and reached down toward his feet. He tinkered with the handcuffs on his left foot until the arm swung open. Keeping his focus, he shifted his weight to his other foot and began to work on the last metal restraint. After a few moments, it opened as well.

Brighton was loose now, but far from free. He gave himself just long enough to let out a deep sigh. Then he quickly picked and pocketed all four pairs of handcuffs.

Brighton slowly stood. His wrists and ankles alternately itched and burned from where the metal cuffs had chafed him. But those minor pains were nothing compared to the soles of his feet. Saenz had whacked them pretty good. Escaping on foot with no boots would be rough, especially since he was being held somewhere in the jungle.

But there was nothing he could do about that except tough it out. He couldn't stay there — not if Saenz intended to focus her next session's punishment on his feet like she'd threatened. As much as his feet stung now, he doubted he'd even be able to walk after a day of thrashings.

Gathering his courage, Brighton walked over to the wall beside the door. He could hear two people murmuring in Spanish outside, so he took out two of the sets of handcuffs he'd collected. With steady hands, he doubled one of them up and stuck his fingers through the loops to hold them like a set of brass knuckles.

Brighton bounced the other pair of handcuffs on his palm for a second. Then he tossed them across the room. The handcuffs struck one of the lights, shattering it. Immediately, the door flew open and two FARC guerillas charged into the room. The guerillas had almost comical looks of shock on their faces at seeing the chair empty. The sight made Brighton grin.

Taking advantage of their confusion, Brighton leapt out from where he was hiding. He punched the man closest to him in the neck with his makeshift brass knuckles. The guerilla staggered, then dropped the M16 he'd been holding. Brighton grabbed the weapon out of the air by the barrel. Then he ducked and spun toward the second man, who was in the process of raising his rifle. Brighton brought the butt of his gun around in a homerun swing.

The butt of the rifle connected with the second guerilla's

stomach. A second swing to the head sent the guerilla flat on his back — and out cold. Brighton quickly did the same to the first guerilla.

With both guerillas down for the count, Brighton pulled the fatigue shirt off one of them. He used the other's belt knife to cut it into two gags. Brighton cuffed the two men together, then cuffed them both to the chair. He wrapped the strips of cloth around their mouths to keep the guerillas quiet in case they woke up soon.

Brighton stuck their knives through his belt, then took the larger man's boots for himself. He pocketed the clip from the first man's M16 and took the other's rifle in his hand. Armed and confident that the two men weren't going anywhere, Brighton decided it was time to leave. Slowly and carefully, he opened the door and stepped outside.

Emerging from the metal and concrete room, Brighton finally had a chance to get his bearings. It was dark out, either early morning or late at night, and quite cooler outside than in the sweatbox he'd been imprisoned in.

Brighton scanned the horizon and saw that the entire area was surrounded by thick jungle. The sound of birds and insects and moving water came from somewhere in the distance. Not too far away, Brighton heard the sound of power tools being used. He could also hear voices, though not well enough to make out what anyone was saying.

Brighton knew he had two choices. First, he could head

directly into the jungle under the cover of darkness and search for running water. Once he found it, he could follow it to either a bigger waterway or straight to civilization — whichever came first. From there, he could find a phone and call in to Shadow Squadron for a pickup.

That first option was certainly the easiest, safest, and most attractive one. After a day like the one he'd spent with Morgan Saenz, the idea of getting caught again made his skin crawl.

His second option was to finish the mission. Weary, beaten, and alone, Brighton was at a serious disadvantage. All the same, he decided to finish the job. After all, the Colombians — and Shadow Squadron — were counting on him. The mission was more important than his comfort or even his safety. And being the youngest member on the squad meant he always had something to prove.

And besides, after what FARC had done to him, Brighton plainly liked the idea of throwing a monkey wrench into the works. With any luck, the air strike would shut down their operation. Maybe for good. So, with a deep breath, Brighton shut the door behind him. Ahead of him was a narrow, trampled path through the jungle. It led off in the direction where Brighton could hear the sounds of power tools and people talking. He began heading that way himself, though he opted to cut through the jungle and move stealthily.

It turned out to be a good choice. As he reached the far end of the path, he saw that it opened onto a compound crawling with FARC guerillas. In groups of two or three, they patrolled or stood near a sprawling one-story building that straddled a wide, straight stretch of muddy river. From within that building came sounds of construction. Trees stood right up against the sides of the building, their branches providing some camouflage from above. The walls had been painted in a brown and green camo pattern as well. There were no exterior lights visible.

It seemed Brighton had found the hidden FARC shipyard after all.

"Lucky me," he muttered.

At least the guerillas had been thoughtful enough to bring him here. Now he just needed to find out where in the world *here* was.

Brighton skirted the tree line in an arc around the central building. He discovered that the shipyard consisted of four structures other than the one-room shed in which he'd spent the previous hours. They included a main construction facility, a wooden barracks for the soldiers and workers, a barn-sized building full of construction supplies, and a smaller place with an antenna on top and its own generator.

That building has to be the command center for the guerilla camp, Brighton thought.

The building wasn't much bigger than the tiny base on Malpelo Island where the rest of Shadow Squadron was holed up. Aside from those buildings, the shipyard also had a row of picnic tables under a tent made of camouflage netting.

There was also a wooden boat dock downstream from the construction building with moored speedboats. A guard watched over it. Another guard sat on a stool next to the one-lane unpaved road leading out into the jungle. Twenty or thirty feet behind that guard, a black off-road motorcycle stood balanced on its kickstand.

Moving slowly in a half-crouch, Brighton made his way toward the command center. He looped through the jungle and came up behind the squat wooden building well out of the guard's line of sight. There were no windows on this side, so all he could do was press his ear to the outside wall and listen. He could hear neither voices nor the sound of people moving around coming from inside. However, he didn't know if that was because no one was inside, or because the walls were just too thick.

In any case, he needed to get inside.

Brighton crept back around the building to the side door that faced the barracks. When he was sure that no one was looking, he darted around the corner and slipped inside.

Brighton closed the door as carefully as he could, but its hinges creaked. In his excited state, Brighton was worried it would give away his position. It was likely that the sound of the generator rumbling on the far side of the building had drowned out the noise, but Brighton froze by the door all the same. He gripped his stolen rifle tightly just in case the nearest guard came by. Only after two tense minutes of silence did Brighton relax and move on.

Inside, the command center wasn't much to look at. It was little more than a long hallway with small rooms on either side and a larger meeting room on the far end. The floor was a poured concrete slab, and the walls and doors were made of thin wood. It was humid, stuffy, and it smelled like old sweat. Still, it wasn't bad for a jungle hideout.

Before him were four doors: two on the left, one at the far end of the hall, and one on the right. The one at the end of the hall was open, showing a dark room with a large table in the center. All sorts of papers were tacked on the walls. To Brighton's right was the front of the building, facing toward the center of the camp. He figured that the door on that side probably led into a living room.

One of the doors on the left was larger than the other. A rim of wan light gleamed around it. Brighton inched down the hall. He stopped outside that door to listen. Luckily, there were no lights on in the hallway to throw his shadow underneath the door. He pointed his rifle at the door and leaned his ear close to the jamb.

The first thing he heard made his blood go cold. It was Saenz's voice. "It's too hard to predict yet," she was saying in Spanish. "He's definitely American special ops of some kind. His equipment was all top of the line, and he's had some torture-resistance training. He's tough. Breaking him will take time."

Judging by the silence afterward, Saenz had to be speaking on the phone to someone. Brighton realized he was shaking a little whenever Saenz spoke. Red, crazy thoughts filled his mind at the sound of his torturer's voice calmly discussing how she'd abused him.

For a moment, Brighton considered simply kicking the door open and letting fly with his rifle on full-auto. He'd give Saenz just enough time to recognize him and realize what was about to happen before he pulled the trigger.

But no . . . he couldn't. For one thing, just opening fire would bring every armed guerilla in the camp running. If that happened, Brighton would end up just as dead as Saenz. Add that to the fact that Brighton had never actually shot anybody before. Sure, he'd caused plenty of very bad guys to die, but only indirectly by calling in fire support from the air. Even when he'd joined his Shadow Squadron teammates on direct-action missions, he'd never actually engaged in the firefights.

But most importantly, Brighton didn't want his first confirmed kill to involve shooting an unarmed woman in cold blood — no matter what she'd done to him.

So Brighton moved on down the hall. The second door on the same side as Saenz's room turned out to be a small closet full of office equipment and medical supplies. The door across the hall that opened toward the front of the building turned out to lead to a small infirmary with a single bed. The front door of the building led directly into the infirmary. Brighton continued down the hall to the last room, with the table in the middle and the papers tacked up on the walls.

Once inside, Brighton grinned. *Jackpot,* he thought. The papers tacked to the walls all proved to be maps. He didn't have sufficient light to read them — the only light in the room was a soft orange glow from the kill switch on a power strip in the corner — but he could at least tell that they were, indeed, maps. There was also a clock on the wall that read *2:15*, which was helpful.

Brighton's eyes lit up with a surge of pure joy when he spotted a very familiar digital-camouflage backpack in the corner. It was his gear, or at least some of it. Forgetting the maps for the moment, he knelt beside his pack and opened the flap. Right on top was his lifeline back to Shadow Squadron: his SINCGARS field radio.

A few other essentials were left in the pack, including some MREs, a first-aid kit, a compass, and a notepad. But the radio was crucial. It almost made up for the loss of his night-vision goggles, his M4 carbine, all his ammunition, his M84 flashbang grenade, and his smoke grenade. At least he hadn't brought his AA-12 combat shotgun with him on this mission. He would have been really depressed if he'd lost his baby.

After a quick inventory, he took a backup flashlight out of the pack, then stuffed everything else back in. He slipped the pack on and switched on the flashlight. With the narrow beam of light, he could read a map without much risk of the enemy spotting him from a distance.

Brighton turned the flashlight on for a second to scan a few of the maps on the walls. After a moment, he selected two to take with him. The first was a fairly new contour map of this part of the jungle, with the location of the guerilla

shipyard conveniently marked. It also showed overland routes for bringing in supplies and river routes for sneaking narco-subs downstream to the ocean.

The second map was a sea chart. It showed the shipping routes off the Colombian coast that the narco-sub pilots took to Mexico. Brighton pulled out the tacks. He folded the chart as quietly as he could, then stuffed it into a cargo pocket. He studied the contour map a few moments before pocketing it along with the flashlight.

Finally, he raised his M16 and made his way back down the hall toward the door where he'd entered the building. Thus far he'd been lucky to avoid detection. But as he approached the door where he'd heard Morgan Saenz talking, the door suddenly opened.

Saenz backed out right into Brighton's path. She held a flashlight in one hand and a book tucked under one arm. When she pulled the door shut, she turned and looked right at Brighton. Fear and anger flashed in her dark eyes. She opened her mouth to shout, but Brighton snapped his rifle up to point at Saenz's neck and shook his head. Saenz immediately closed her mouth.

Brighton jerked his head to the side, motioning for Saenz to go back into the room. Saenz did as she was told, and Brighton followed her into what turned out to be her living quarters. It had a footlocker, a desk with a laptop computer, and a twin bed under a mosquito-net canopy. There was a stack of books in the corner next to the desk. A pair of citronella candles provided dim light.

Saenz turned to face Brighton. "You'll never escape," she said.

"Sit down," Brighton said flatly, nodding toward the bed. She did so, never taking her eyes off his.

Brighton took out one of the remaining pairs of handcuffs and tossed it onto the bed next to Saenz. "Cuff your ankle to the bedframe," Brighton ordered her.

Saenz narrowed her eyes but did as he said. "I only have to yell, young man," she said, "and every FARC soldier in this camp will come to my aid. You might kill me for it, but you won't live long enough to enjoy it."

Brighton smiled at her, his eyes hard as he glared at her over the M16's iron sights. "Go ahead, sister," he challenged. "Yell your head off."

Saenz glared back at him. Then she lowered her eyes. "So now what?" she asked.

"I'm leaving," Brighton said. "I ought to take you prisoner, but that sounds like more trouble than you're worth. You'll probably just jump off the boat the second I take my eyes off you, anyway. So you get to stay here, but don't you dare think I'll ever forget about you, Señora Saenz."

Brighton backed out into the hallway and paused. His rifle never wavered, but his mind wasn't so steady. He so badly wanted to pull the trigger and erase Saenz from the world. Who knew how many others would suffer at her hands. And he knew she was just going to raise the alarm and bring everybody running the second he was out of her sight. He might as well get the satisfaction of killing her now while he had the chance.

But he couldn't. While it might satisfy him to destroy the one who'd hurt him and who knows how many others, Brighton just couldn't bring himself to do it. He had to rise above those impulses if he wanted to be able to look at himself in the mirror tomorrow. He had to be better than the enemy if he wanted to be able to call himself one of the good guys. There was nothing else he could do.

Without another word, he turned and bolted for the side door. He hit it and darted around the corner of the building, desperately hoping that no one happened to be looking his way. It took only that long for Saenz to gather her courage and yell.

"The American has escaped!" she shouted in Spanish. "He's going for the boats! Cut him off!"

Hearing Saenz's shout made Brighton smile. *Sucker,* he thought.

Brighton continued to move along the rear of the building toward the motorcycle on the other side. Saenz kept shouting inside, and the guard who'd been posted on the stool by the one-lane jungle road ran back toward the dock. He shouted for everyone else to be on the lookout. All the guerillas in earshot sprang into action and fanned out to search. But they were looking in the wrong direction.

Brighton got to the bike to find the keys in the ignition, as he expected. He slung his rifle over one shoulder, hopped on the bike, and kicked it to life. The sound of the engine

drew the guerillas' attention like a magnet — and silenced Saenz's yelling for a second. But no one was close enough to do anything to stop him.

Brighton hit the headlight and tore off down the supply road. Some of the guards came running and fired a few shots after him, but the bullets pinged harmlessly off nearby trees.

No one could stop him now.

* * *

A short while later, morning sunlight illuminated the jungle's canopy. Brighton had long since ditched his stolen motorcycle. Now, he set off overland with his map to find high ground and take the lay of the terrain.

Lying on his belly on a ridge with the guerillas' map beside him, he glanced down at the river that passed through the middle of the FARC camp. He couldn't see the camouflaged shipyard from here, but he knew the geography and landmarks well enough to know exactly where it lay. He set his field radio to the Shadow Squadron's emergency frequency and keyed the transmitter.

"Aerie, this is Eagle," Brighton said, using their callsigns. "Aerie, this is Eagle. Do you read me?"

"Eagle!" Lieutenant Commander Ryan Cross answered at once. His voice was full of surprise, delight, and relief. "Eagle, this is Aerie. Give me a status report. Are you all right?"

"I've been better, Commander," Brighton said. "And I'm going to need an airlift here pretty soon."

"The Osprey's already in the air, Eagle," Cross said. "We've been looking for you."

"Good to hear it, Aerie," Brighton said. "But if it's all the same, I need to connect to Major Gaitan first. Little matter of an air strike I promised him."

"Fair enough, Eagle," Cross replied, clearly impressed. "Make your call. We'll be here."

"Roger that," Brighton chirped. "See you soon, sir. Eagle out."

"Good work out there, Eagle," Cross said. "I knew we could count on you. Aerie out."

Brighton pocketed his radio. "You have no idea, man," he said softly. "No idea."

MISSION DEBRIEFING

OPERATION

EAGLE DOWN

1234

MISSION COMPLETE

PRIMARY OBJECTIVE

- Covert insertion via parachute

- Rendezvouz with Colombian task force

- Locate shipyard

- Call in coordinates for precision air strike

SECONDARY OBJECTIVES

- Minimize casualties

x Foster positive relations with
  Colombian task force

x Remain undetected

STATUS

5/7 COMPLETE

BRIGHTON, EDGAR

RANK: Staff Sergeant
BRANCH: Air Force Combat Controller
PSYCH PROFILE: The team's technician and close-quarters-combat specialist is popular with his squadmates but often agitates his commanding officers.

I've been putting off writing this debriefing, mostly because I'm still sorting out everything that happened to me. Between the waterboarding, the stun-gunning, and my interrogator's lousy sense of humor, I was pushed to my breaking point — and beyond. But I trusted in my training, which is the only reason I'm still alive . . . well, that and the ballpoint pen. As for Morgan Saenz, she was picked up a few days ago by the Colombian task force. One guess as to who tipped them off that she'd be heading back to Mexico.

\- Staff Sergeant Edgar Brighton

ZOI9.681

MISSION BRIEFING

OPERATION

SNIPER SHIELD 1234

I've been given a rather unpleasant VIP protection mission. I'll be guarding a man named Heshem Shadid, an Iraqi politician. Admittedly, Shadid is a valuable asset to the war effort. He has given useful intel to US forces on several occasions. Unfortunately, Shadid is also a former terrorist.

Obviously, Shadid's old friends are none too pleased that he has switched sides, and they'll do anything to take him out. It's my job to stop them.

— Lieutenant Kimiyo Yamashita

3245.98

IRAQ

PRIMARY OBJECTIVES

- Meet with the VIP and his personal security force

- Prep a route and determine an overwatch position for transit

- Protect the VIP en route to his destination

SECONDARY OBJECTIVES

- Avoid open conflict with Iraqi insurgents

- Keep our presence covert

1932.789

0412.981

1624.054

SNIPER SHIELD

Shadow Squadron was in Iraq and had been operating there for the past several weeks. Officially, the US-led war had been over for years, and the last of the American combat forces had withdrawn months ago. Iraq, however, was still a bed of chaos. Terrorist organizations and local militias continued to stir up endless problems for the newly elected government. The remaining internal threats were so severe that even the locals admitted they weren't ready to handle them on their own. So they called on their American allies for help — namely, Shadow Squadron.

Lieutenant Commander Cross glanced up at the sun and shielded his eyes. The blistering heat in Nasiriyah, in southeastern Iraq, was intense. The searing sun and extremely dry air were impossible to ignore. But in the midst of an operation, with death hiding around every corner or lurking in every shadow, there wasn't time for distractions. Mental lapses could prove to be fatal. Besides, for the members of Shadow Squadron, it took much more than extreme temperatures or physical discomfort to affect their focus.

For the most part, Shadow Squadron's assistance in Iraq had involved training local military forces or providing protection for local VIPs who didn't yet trust their own soldiers. Occasionally, Cross and his men were given direct-action assignments like live-fire raids on hostile targets. Like today.

Acting on a tip from a trusted politician from the Dhi Qar Province, Cross's eight-man squad was tasked with an assault on an al-Qaeda insurgent cell. The cell was currently holed up in an abandoned apartment complex in Nasiriyah. According to the tip, they were planning to sneak bombs into the drainage pump station along the Euphrates River. Intel confirmed that the cell had been stockpiling explosives in their hideout for months.

The Nasiriyah station was the largest in the Middle East. It was likely that the insurgents hoped to disable a vital public structure. Or to strike fear into the hearts of the locals. Either way, Cross had decided that now was the time to act.

Shadow Squadron's black Seahawk helicopter roared in low over the skyline. It briefly paused over the abandoned apartment building. Almost immediately, six members of Shadow Squadron fast-roped down onto the roof. The chopper then hopped over to another building across the street. There, two more team members, Brighton and Yamashita, dropped in. These two would act as overwatch for the rest of the team, picking off any insurgents who tried to escape.

So far, the operation was proceeding smoothly. Cross and Walker led the six-man squad down into the building. They made their way through the structure slowly, checking blind spots and covering each other's backs. They encountered no resistance — until they reached the ground floor. Cross and his men had caught the insurgents in the middle of lunch. To say they were caught unprepared would be a massive understatement.

Cross grinned, and then squeezed the trigger of his M4 carbine. He fired a single round into the ceiling as a warning shot.

One of the Iraqis sprinted out of the room. The rest of the insurgents fell over themselves trying to surrender. Cross motioned for Walker and Sergeant Mark Shepherd to join him in pursuit of the fleeing hostile. The remaining three members of Shadow Squadron stayed behind to secure the noncombatants.

Cross chased the fleeing insurgent down a hall and around a corner. Suddenly, the insurgent popped out from a half-open door with an AK-47 in his hand. The Iraqi sprayed bullets wildly down the hallway at Cross and his men.

Ducking out of harm's way just in time, Cross reached around the corner with his rifle to throw out suppressing fire. The spray forced the Iraqi back into his hole, and also bought enough time for Walker and Shepherd to rush around the corner and get into cover positions down the hallway.

When the insurgent stuck his head out to see once again, he was surprised to see all three Americans open fire. Chief Walker managed to hit the Iraqi in the side by firing straight through the cheap drywall beside the door frame. At the same

time, a one-in-a-million shot from Cross popped the insurgent in the wrist.

The injured man's rifle skittered down the hallway as he retreated back into the room. Before Walker could close in on him, the Iraqi kicked the door shut. Then he locked it.

Cross, Walker, and Shepherd huddled together just outside the locked door. Walker and Shepherd glanced at Cross for orders. Cross took a position to the left of the door and motioned Walker to the opposite side. He signaled for Shepherd to get ready to kick the door in, but then gestured for him to hold position.

Cross tapped the small button on the two-way canalphone tucked into his right ear. "Fireteam Two, report," Cross said, whispering just loud enough for the tiny earbud radio to pick up his voice.

"All clear here, sir," Staff Sergeant Paxton replied on the line. "The only man not accounted for is the one you went after."

"Good, we'll bring him around," Cross answered quietly. "Out." He paused for a moment to let the line clear, then tapped his canalphone again. "Overwatch, report."

"No rats, sir," Brighton reported. He was stationed on the roof across the street with Yamashita, the team's sniper.

While Yamashita scanned the building and the street through the Leupold scope of his M110 sniper rifle, Brighton scanned the area through the high-resolution camera on his remote-controlled reconnaissance UAV quad-copter. "No sign of reinforcements, either."

"Good," Cross replied. "Out."

"Wait," Yamashita said. "Your fugitive is holed up in a room on the south face of the building, right?"

Cross took a moment to check his relative position in the building. "Affirmative," Cross said. "Do you have a visual on our target?"

"I can tell which room he went into, but I don't have a shot from this vantage point," Yamashita said. "I'm relocating now."

"Roger that," Cross said. "Out."

"Sir," Walker said when comm-traffic in the team's earphones stopped. He nodded toward the closed door between them and the wounded insurgent. "Let me try to talk to him. I can get him to come out."

Shepherd looked skeptical but didn't say anything. Cross had his doubts, too.

"He can't be more than eighteen years old, sir," Walker said, reading their expressions. "He's been shot twice already and he's probably scared to death. Let me give him a chance to surrender with his dignity intact. He'll take it."

Cross knew all about the chief's optimistic faith in humanity and how it occasionally clouded his judgment. However, Cross didn't like the idea of kicking in the door and gunning down a scared teenager any more than Walker did. So, with a nod, Cross motioned toward the door. He kept his M4 ready, though, as did Shepherd.

"Son, I want you to listen to me," Walker spoke in Arabic, leaning toward the door. "I know you're in pain, and I know you're losing blood. I know you're scared. But if you work with me, I can get you out of this mess without —"

"I have a way out!" the insurgent barked back.

The desperation in the boy's voice made Cross nervous, but at least it gave him a good sense of where he was standing. Cross exchanged a look with Shepherd, making sure the Green Beret would be ready to breach the door. Shepherd nodded.

"Let's talk about this," Walker said, his voice calm and steady, as if he were talking to one of his own kids back home. "What's your name?"

"Don't pretend you care who I am," the insurgent snarled in Arabic. "All you care about is —"

The boy's words stopped short as a muffled thump sounded from within the room. Cross thought he'd heard a sound like glass breaking but not shattering. Everything was silent. Cross didn't like that. Ignoring the frustration on Walker's face, Cross signaled Shepherd to breach the door.

Shepherd launched himself across the hall and bashed the door off its hinges with a powerful kick. Cross and Walker were right on his heels as the three of them spread out to cover the room in all directions. No sooner were they through the door when Yamashita's voice came over their canalphones. "Clear," the sniper said.

"Clear," Cross confirmed. Walker and Shepherd spread out to check the rooms on both sides. They both reported clear.

As Walker and Shepherd returned, Cross assessed the state of the room. Except for sturdy tables in each corner, the room had no furniture. A single window dominated the wall opposite the door. It had a small hole in it near the top, surrounded by a spiderweb of hairline cracks.

The insurgent lay in the center of the floor, sprawled on his face with his knees tucked under him. A dark stain was spreading out across the carpet beneath him. To Cross's shock, the boy looked up at him. He was opening and closing his mouth as if he were trying to speak.

"He's alive!" Walker gasped. He tapped his earphone as he crouched by the kid's side. "Medic! We need you up here now."

"On my way," Kyle Williams replied.

"Cancel that, Williams," Cross said. He met Chief Walker's wild, angry eyes with perfect calm.

"Sir," Williams said, signing off.

"He's not going to make it, Chief," Cross said to Walker. "There's nothing we can do for him now."

"Fine," Walker said. He glanced down and saw that the insurgent was already dead. "But Yamashita and I are going to have a long talk later."

"Maybe you should put him in for a medal," Shepherd suggested in a low, respectful tone.

Walker glared angrily at Shepherd. Shepherd simply pointed below and nudged the fallen boy's outstretched right hand with the toe of his boot. Walker saw a gunmetal-gray device in the Iraqi's limp hand.

Only then did Walker take a good look around the room to see what Cross and Shepherd had already noticed. In all four corners of the room, on and under the tables, were stacked blocks of black market plastic explosives. One of the blocks on the table nearest the boy had an electronic detonator jammed into it. That one block alone would have killed everyone in the room.

"If all of those explosive had gone off," Shepherd said, "the explosion would have easily destroyed the building. Along with us inside it."

* * *

Several hours later, back at base, Shadow Squadron had squared away their gear and finished their after-action reports. As Cross entered the barracks, he saw that Walker was yelling at Yamashita.

"The kill wasn't necessary," Walker insisted. "I could've talked him down."

"I didn't know you were talking to him at all, Chief," Yamashita said. "I just saw him pick up that trigger and start waving it around."

As always, Yamashita was calm. Cross noted, however, that Walker was anything but composed. Even still, Cross waited and listened before intervening.

"What if it'd been a dead-man switch?" Walker demanded. "You would've brought that whole building down!"

Cross had to admit that was a good point. That kind of trigger would've been armed the moment the insurgent squeezed it, but wouldn't have gone off unless the insurgent let go.

"It wasn't a dead-man switch," Yamashita said.

"You could tell?" Cross asked.

"Sir," Yamashita replied with a nod. At the time, he'd been only about eighty percent sure. But Yamashita decided that Walker and Cross didn't need to know that.

"He was hurt and scared, Lieutenant," Walker said, returning to his original point. "I could've gotten him to surrender. Nobody had to die. Especially not like that. I mean, you shot him in the throat."

Yamashita hadn't known that until now. "I was shooting through glass," Yamashita said, his voice calm and even. "I was aiming for his chest. Some deflection is unavoidable, even at that range."

"It was avoidable," Walker snapped. "You didn't have to take the shot! I mean, nobody ordered you to. If you hadn't jumped the gun, that boy would still be alive!"

Yamashita suppressed a shudder of rage. He started to say something, but Cross interrupted. "All right, Walker," Cross said. "You've made your position more than clear. It's time to let me handle this."

"Sir, I —" Walker began.

"Chief," Cross said, cutting him off. "I got it."

Walker was not satisfied, but he put up no further argument. He gave Yamashita one last cold look then stormed out of the room.

"Follow me, Lieutenant," Cross said. He led Yamashita to the room that served as his office while Shadow Squadron was stationed there.

Yamashita understood where Walker was coming from, but the chief always believed he could save the world if he just tried hard enough. Walker had no idea what Yamashita had to deal with every time he pulled the trigger on his M110.

Cross sat down in the chair behind his wooden desk. He gestured for Yamashita to take the stool across from him. "Walker's pretty salty right now," Cross said. "Keep in mind that he's not angry at you. It's just the situation that bothers him."

Yamashita glanced through the open blinds on the window behind Cross. In the distance, he could see the massive Ziggurat of Ur that lay within the security perimeter of the air base. The ancient pile of bricks was over forty centuries old. It would still be there when the Iraqis and Americans were only a memory. "I know how Walker is," Yamashita finally said.

"Officially, you made the right call," Cross said. "I would have ordered you to take the shot. Next time, though, I need to know what you know. When you're on overwatch, you have to keep me informed of any new information you find."

Yamashita didn't reply, but some of what he was thinking must have shown on his face. Cross raised an eyebrow. "Something on your mind, Lieutenant?" Cross asked. "You can speak freely."

Yamashita hesitated. His previous commanding officer had said the exact same thing only to bait a trap. Cross didn't seem like the type, though. Yamashita decided to take the opportunity.

"I know I should have told you as soon as I saw the C4 blocks on the tables," Yamashita said, looking at Cross's desk. "I was about to, but when that guy stuck the detonator in and picked up that trigger, I didn't think I had time. So I took the shot."

Cross narrowed his eyes. "That's fair," he said. "Just don't make a habit out of it."

Yamashita met Cross's eyes directly with his own. "Yes, sir," he said.

Cross nodded, satisfied with the response. "While I've got you here, is there anything else you need to talk about?" Cross asked. "I keep an open-door policy for my team."

"No, sir," Yamashita said immediately, even though it was a tempting offer. He stood and folded his hands behind his back. "If that's all . . ."

"Sure, you're dismissed," Cross said. He tapped his temple with his finger. "But if things start piling up in here, I need to know about it."

"Sir," Yamashita said. This time, Yamashita could see that Cross wasn't pleased by his one-word answer, but it was the best Yamashita could manage at the moment.

Yamashita lingered for a moment. Then he saluted and left.

* * *

Within a week, Shadow Squadron had another local assignment. Cross called his team together in a conference room at Tallil Air Base. Staff Sergeant Brighton synced up a tablet computer with a palm-sized projector. It shone on the wall opposite the door.

The six squad soldiers sat around the conference table. Cross and Chief Walker stood at the front of the room on opposite sides of the projected computer display. For the moment, the screen displayed the swords-and-globe emblem of the Joint Special Operations Command.

"Morning," Cross said with a nod to the team. "We've got a situation developing with one of our human intelligence assets in Dhi Qar province. He's the same guy who's been feeding us all of our recent intel about insurgent activities. He believes he's been targeted for assassination, so he's asked us to supplement his private security force at a special event two days from now."

"He asked for us?" Yamashita asked, his eyes narrowed.

"He actually asked his CIA handler, Agent Bradley Upton," Cross clarified. "Upton's Special Activities Division unit is stretched thin, so we've been asked to help them out."

"Why are we doing a favor for the CIA?" Brighton asked.

Cross shrugged. "That's above my pay grade," he said. Yamashita thought the commander didn't look all too happy about this particular favor.

"So who's the asset?" Brighton asked.

"His name is Heshem Shadid," Cross replied.

Cross tapped on the tablet. An image of a middle-aged Iraqi man in an expensive suit popped up. He had a deep widow's peak of iron-gray hair. "Shadid is a recent addition to the Iraqi parliament in the Prime Minister's Islamic Dawa Party. Apparently, he's been with al-Dawa since the Iran—Iraq War in the 1980s."

"Loyal," Brighton murmured, impressed. "The '80s and '90s weren't good times to be al-Dawa."

In Yamashita's opinion, Brighton had entirely missed the point. In the 1980s, during the Iran—Iraq war, al-Dawa had been a terrorist organization devoted to promoting the Islamic religion. It had supported Iran's Islamic Revolution and received support from that country for efforts against the Baathists in Iraq. After a host of al-Dawa terrorist activities, including the bombing of the US embassy in Kuwait in 1983, the Baathists had all but wiped out the remaining al-Dawa members. The few who survived the crackdown had either fled the country or gone into hiding. It wasn't until the fall of Saddam Hussein's brutal regime that the Baathists fell from power, which made it safe for the al-Dawa members to finally resurface.

Loyal or not, al-Dawa had still committed terrorist acts against their own people. In Yamashita's opinion, they didn't deserve sympathy.

"In two days," Cross continued, "Shadid will be attending an exhibition soccer match at the An Nasiriyah Stadium. He's giving a speech before the match, hoping to earn popular support for his party."

"At least he'll have a captive audience," Brighton joked.

"That's enough, Brighton," Walker growled, apparently fed up with the chatter. Yamashita was getting a little tired of it himself. He liked Brighton, but the young soldier's lack of focus was distracting sometimes.

"Sorry, Chief," Brighton said.

Cross swiped the tablet's touch screen, bringing up a street map of Nasiriyah. One route blinked in red. "This is the route Shadid will follow from his place to the stadium, along with alternates. Agent Upton's SAD unit will be on station at the house and at the stadium, coordinating with Shadid's personal security men. Our job is to secure the route and ride with Shadid. He'll be traveling in his armored limo, and we've got our van. We'll use Brighton's UAV for aerial recon."

Cross glanced at Yamashita and added. "We'll set you up midway for overwatch."

"Is there a specific threat against this guy?" the team's newest member, Second Lieutenant Aram Jannati, asked. Jannati had come out of the Marine Special Operations

Regiment, replacing the deceased Neil Larssen. "Why do we believe he's been targeted for assassination?"

Cross swiped a few times on his tablet. "The day after his people issued the press release that said Shadid would be at An Nasiriyah Stadium, he received this picture in an unmarked envelope," the commander said.

Another photo of Shadid appeared. But this one had been altered. It showed Shadid getting out of his limo in front of the Baghdad Convention Center, which was where the Parliament met. In the picture, Shadid's left eye had been blacked out with a marker. Arabic letters had been drawn on his forehead.

Shepherd slowly frowned. "'Infidel,'" he said, interpreting the letters written on the picture. "That's not good."

"Infidel is *kafira*, with an alif," Walker corrected. "This says *kefira*. It means 'disbelief.'"

"On the back of the picture," Cross said, advancing to a new image on his tablet, "this word was written in marker." Printed neatly on the back of the photo in Arabic was the word *Zulfiqar*.

"Oh," Jannati said. "I see."

Yamashita didn't understand. Frowns on the rest of the men's faces told him that he was not alone. Cross motioned for Jannati to explain. "Zulfiqar is the name of the Blade of Evil's Bane," Jannati said. "'*On the day of judgment, the Twelfth Imam will strike down the Deceiving Messiah.*' Zulfiqar is the sword he will use to kill him." He paused, then shrugged. "Or so the story goes, anyway."

Brighton rolled his eyes. "So our VIP is targeted for assassination by a guy using the name Zulfiqar," he said dryly.

Walker nodded. "Yes, it fits. According to the legends, that is how the Deceiving Messiah can be recognized. That, and the fact that he'll be trying to drive people away from an Islamic state."

"Do people think Shadid is doing that?" Jannati asked.

"Depends on who you ask," Cross said. "There are some who don't like the fact that Shadid and his party are disarming the militias. Some believe that disarming the militias is a step on the road back to a secular, or nonreligious, state."

"That sounds like an excuse to fight for political power," Yamashita said with distaste in his voice.

"That's Agent Upton's read on it, too," Cross answered. "From what Upton's people have gathered, this Zulfiqar business is just to put fear into Shadid's enemies. At its heart, though, this threat on Shadid's life is about nothing more than politics, power, and money."

"So it's just another sunny day in Iraq," Brighton said.

Some of the other men chuckled, but Yamashita didn't laugh. It wasn't funny — it was disgusting. His team was being asked to stand in harm's way — to potentially kill — people in order to protect a former terrorist and traitor. Yamashita had joined the military because he wanted to protect America from its enemies, not to protect bad guys from their enemies. Unfortunately, that turned out to be their job all too often.

And Yamashita was getting sick of it.

* * *

Two hours after the briefing, Yamashita was dressed and ready for work. He sat in the passenger seat of a borrowed vehicle as Lieutenant Commander Cross drove all the main and backup routes Shadid could possibly take to An Nasiriyah Stadium at week's end.

Every once in a while, Yamashita signaled Cross to stop. Then he aimed out the window with a high-tech laser rangefinding apparatus. He used the rangefinder to check lines of sight and measure distances from the road to various firing positions that overlooked it. He'd already picked a few potential overwatch positions on the first trip from Shadid's front gate to the stadium. But Yamashita needed the fresh perspective of each trip to help him make up his mind.

He also needed the extra time to try to reconsider his own perspective on the mission, as well as the life he'd chosen by joining Shadow Squadron.

Yamashita put down the rangefinder. The car got moving again. "What do you think?" Cross asked.

"The southeast corner room on the top floor of that building should do," Yamashita said, looking out the window.

"That one?" Cross asked, leaning over briefly to look out Yamashita's passenger-side window. "You sure?" He pointed to a taller building down the block and said, "That one's taller. Looks like a better field of view over the backup routes we might need to take through this part of town, too."

Yamashita met Cross's eyes and cocked an eyebrow. "With all due respect, Commander . . ."

Cross laughed. "All right, Lieutenant, I get it," he said. "You're the one with the sniper training. I trust your judgment."

"Sir," Yamashita said.

"You know, after I got my commission, I applied to sniper school," Cross said. "I didn't get in, though."

"No?" Yamashita said. "I've seen you shoot. What happened?"

"My CO at the time denied me," Cross said. "He wanted me fast-tracked for command, and he was worried that being a sniper would derail my career."

"He probably did you a favor," Yamashita said.

Cross perked up, making Yamashita wish he'd held his tongue. "Why?" Cross asked.

Yamashita hesitated. "It suits some better than others," he said with a shrug.

"Oh?" Cross asked. "How does it suit you, Lieutenant?"

Yamashita frowned. He looked down at the rangefinder resting on his knees. He saw he was clenching the side of the device so hard that his knuckles were turning white. He forced himself to relax his grip.

After about a minute of silence, Cross finally pulled the vehicle they'd borrowed over onto the side of the road. He turned halfway around in his seat to look squarely at Yamashita.

"Talk to me, Lieutenant," he said. "You've had a black cloud over your head since the mission briefing."

Yamashita knew that stubborn silence at a moment like this would only cause more problems in the long run. He took a breath to collect his thoughts. When he finally found the same calm that he summoned whenever he pulled the trigger on his M110, he spoke. "I read Upton's report on Shadid after the meeting," he said. "He's a piece of garbage, our VIP. All these 'tips' he's been giving us on insurgents are all on his former associates. They are people he worked with when he was a terrorist. He sells them out to the CIA, and we go wipe them out. But if you look at it closely, a few years ago he was doing the kinds of things they are now."

Cross's face looked like he'd just tasted something unpleasant. He couldn't deny what Yamashita was saying, so he just nodded.

"So why should Shadid get a free ride when these other guys don't?" Yamashita asked. "Why does he get to play politics with one hand while signing his old friends' death warrants with the other?"

"Because he's got what it takes to play the game," Cross said. "Shadid — and all the rest like him — were the first and loudest to step up and promise they could help us turn Iraq into a democracy. He's using his dark past to help us build a bright future for this country."

"His past is that he's a terrorist and a criminal," Yamashita said. His voice was as steady as his trigger finger. His thoughts, however, were anything but calm. "He doesn't care about the future. He just wants whatever power, money, and influence he can grab."

"True," Cross said with a sigh. "But where would this country be right now if not for opportunists like him? Think about the mission earlier this week. If not for the intel Shadid provided, we'd never have known what that cell was planning. Think of the damage they could have done."

Yamashita knew Cross had a point, but it made the situation no easier to accept. "I know, I know, Commander," Yamashita said. "That's just the way things work here —"

"Not just here," Cross cut in. "This isn't any different from how lawyers back home make plea bargains with criminals to catch other, more dangerous criminals. As distasteful as it is, sometimes it's just better to let one scumbag go free if it gets a whole gang of scumbags off the street."

"I understand the logic, Commander," Yamashita said. "It makes me wonder whether we're actually doing long-term good, or just creating bigger problems for the next generation to deal with. Just like the last generation did for us."

"I wish I had the right answer, Lieutenant," Cross said. "But there just isn't one. The best we can do is focus on the small details about our jobs. That's all we have any control over."

"The small details," Yamashita repeated.

The sniper lapsed back into silence. He wasn't sure what he'd been expecting Cross to say, but "lock it down and walk it off" wasn't it. He was already trying to deal with things by focusing on the small scale. Doing his job — especially on overwatch — was all about focusing on the small scale. The flow of battle might change completely when he pulled the trigger, but it was easy to lose sight of that in the rifle scope. For him, combat occurred one bullet, one target, one shot at a time.

That was the heart of the problem now. Fate had let an evil man escape the punishment that Yamashita himself had doled out to that young al-Qaeda insurgent. That boy with the bomb. No matter what Walker said, that kid deserved to be taken out. Why, then, should Shadid get away with all the evil things he'd done?

If Shadid doesn't deserve to live, Yamashita wondered, *am I truly obligated to do everything I can to protect the man's life?*

Yamashita certainly wouldn't shoot Shadid himself. But by not pulling the trigger — by not saving Shadid from those who wanted to kill him — maybe he could do the work that fate had apparently forgotten.

Maybe it was just that simple.

* * *

On the day of the soccer match and the politician's speech, Shadow Squadron traveled in the pre-dawn hours to Shadid's compound in Nasiriyah. It was a walled sandstone fortress that had escaped all damage from the fierce fighting in the US-led war. A pair of guards — one local man and one American SAD operative — met them at the gate. It took the guards about five minutes to clear them before their cars rolled inside.

Bradley Upton, the CIA agent who worked with Shadid, was there to greet them. Upton wore khakis and a button-down shirt with the sleeves rolled up to his elbows. He shook hands with each member of the Shadow Squadron team. Yamashita had no doubt that Upton was an experienced and competent field operative. However, his first impression of the man was that he looked like a middle-aged used car salesman. The agent's slick smile didn't do anything to dispel the image, either.

"Commander, I'm glad you could make it!" Upton said with far too much enthusiasm. "The CIA appreciates the loan of your men and the use of your time."

"It wasn't my call," Cross answered. "Is there somewhere we can set up?"

"Right this way," Upton said, gesturing his arm with a flourish. If Upton took offense to Cross's comment, he didn't show it. "Shadid's waiting for us in the dining room."

Yamashita followed the team out of the foyer, then down a long hall to a set of mahogany doors that led into Heshem Shadid's dining room. The long table down the center was set for coffee, with trays of fruit at every seat. Heshem sat at one end of the table with the head of his security staff on his left. There was an empty chair on his right. When Upton entered the room, he headed for that chair. Shadid rose and met him halfway.

"Heshem," Upton said, "this is the rest of my security detail. They'll be handling your en-route security today."

Yamashita saw Cross scowl at Upton's description of his team. But the commander put on his professional demeanor and shook Shadid's hand with a smile.

"Mr. Upton assures me your men are very talented," Shadid said to Cross in English. "We're looking forward to a safe journey."

Cross cocked his head at that. Upton's eyes narrowed just a little. "We, sir?" Cross asked. He looked at Upton. "Is there something we don't know?"

"A change of plans," Upton admitted. "Mister Shadid's ten-year-old grandson will be joining you today."

A faint electric charge seemed to move through the men of Shadow Squadron. All of them froze for a moment and perked up.

Cross glanced quickly from Upton to Shadid. "What's this about?" he asked, his voice flat over suppressed annoyance. Yamashita had heard the commander use the same tone on Walker plenty of times.

"Habib is a great fan of Younis Mahmoud, the captain of our national soccer team," Shadid explained. "I promised him the chance to meet him after the game."

"That's fine," Cross said diplomatically. "But we should arrange to get him there separately."

"Nonsense," Shadid said, brushing the suggestion away with the back of his hand. "If you can keep me safe, you can keep us both safe."

"It's an unnecessary risk," Cross said.

"Quite the opposite," Shadid said. "I've made it known all week that Habib would be accompanying me to this engagement. By now, Zulfiqar's assassins undoubtedly have heard. From what I know of them from Mr. Upton, I believe these men are not careless or barbaric. They won't risk taking Habib's life in an attempt to assassinate me."

"You can't be sure of that," Cross said through clenched teeth.

"I have the full faith that comes from my trust in your country," Shadid replied. Yamashita saw a flicker of a smug smile on the former terrorist's face. "I'm sure that having Habib with me will be the safest thing for both of us. Zulfiqar and his men might still make an attempt on my life. However, his honor will force them to take greater care not to harm any innocents. They will be bound by that honor, and that will make them easier for you to deal with."

"Did honor ever constrain you from harming innocents?" Yamashita muttered.

"You're referring to my . . . past?" Shadid said. He turned his cold, lifeless eyes at Yamashita. "You can be certain, young man, that I am nothing like the man I used to be."

Yamashita looked up to find Cross, Chief Walker, and Agent Upton staring at him. Upton and Cross's expressions were unreadable. Walker, however, was glaring at him with the same look of death he gave Brighton's dumb jokes. Yamashita nodded at Shadid, then shut his mouth.

"Mr. Upton and I have already talked about this," Shadid said to Cross. "Habib is coming with me. That ends the discussion."

"The customer's always right," Upton said, shrugging mock-apologetically to Cross.

"All right," Cross said. "It doesn't really change the plan — it just raises the stakes. So let's look at the routes."

At a signal from Cross, Brighton set up the palm projector on the table. The members of Shadow Squadron took up positions around the room. Cross broke out the tablet computer and began paging through the presentation he'd designed the day before. Upton had already signed off on it via e-mail, and now Shadid nodded along with all the key points without arguing. He had gotten his way with regard to bringing his grandson along, so it seemed he was prepared to be reasonable about everything else.

Listening quietly to the plan he'd already committed to memory, Yamashita couldn't take his mind off Shadid. He hadn't meant to say anything to the man, but the politician's gall and cowardice had surprised him. In Yamashita's mind, bringing a kid along in hopes of making criminal terrorists less likely to act was the height of complete stupidity. But the fact that Upton had agreed to it in the first place must have meant that Shadid was an intelligence asset of the utmost importance.

Even if Shadid was right about bringing his grandson along, what he was doing was no better than holding the boy up in front of himself as a human shield. That the man was willing to risk a child's life to protect his own only confirmed Yamashita's opinion of Shadid. For a moment, he was tempted to walk out of the room in protest. Or maybe "lose track" of Shadid en route to the event.

Yamashita's thoughts chased each other in his head as he half-listened to Cross's presentation. At the end, Upton brought the newcomers up to speed about what his unit would be doing and how they'd be coordinating with Shadid's small personal security force. Yamashita took mental notes, but none of that information affected his job, so he allowed himself to get lost in thought. He returned to full attention when Cross took control of the meeting again.

"Here's how we'll roll out," the commander said. He looked from Williams to Chief Walker. "Chief, you and the corpsman will ride in the limo with Shadid, Agent Upton, and the head of Mister Shadid's security."

"Sir," Walker and Williams said.

"You'll drive the van," Cross said to Staff Sergeant Paxton. Paxton nodded. Cross looked at Brighton next. "You'll ride shotgun and operate the UAV to keep us informed and connected."

"Sir," Brighton said, smiling proudly. No doubt he liked the idea of riding shotgun. It gave him the chance to break out his baby — an AA-12 combat shotgun.

"I want you two in the back of the van," Cross said to Shepherd and Jannati. To Shepherd, he said, "You're in the hot seat." He looked at Jannati. "You're on ammo and support."

"Sir," the soldiers replied. Shepherd wore a huge grin. Jannati looked glum and disappointed. "Privilege of seniority, sir," Shepherd told the Marine. Although Jannati had more experience in the field, Shepherd had been with Shadow Squadron longer.

"And you're with me on overwatch," Cross said, finally addressing Yamashita. "We'll head out first and set up in the spot you picked yesterday." He looked at Walker. "When we're in position, I'll give you the go-ahead."

"Sir," Walker said.

"I'll get my teams in position," Upton said. "We'll go live on your signal, Commander."

"My men will take their orders from yours," Shadid said to Upton. He then opened his arms wide in a gesture that took in Cross and Upton and said, "I can't thank you both enough for this."

"We're just doing our jobs, Shadid," Upton said.

"Gear up and get ready to move out," Cross said to his team, ignoring Shadid entirely. He looked at Yamashita and said, "Lieutenant, you're with me."

"Sir," Yamashita replied. He turned and followed Cross out. On the way, he stole one last glance at Heshem Shadid.

* * *

The sun was just coming up when Cross and Yamashita took their places in the overwatch position. They built a sniper nest in the corner room of an empty seven-story building. The structure had taken a great deal of damage during the Battle of Nasiriyah. The room they'd chosen was missing its roof and part of the wall at the corner, which gave them a commanding view of the route below as well as the buildings across the street. It also offered cover from any firing position from seven stories and below.

Yamashita assembled his M110 sniper rifle while Cross hung a sheet of sand-colored netting across the widest gaps in the broken wall. The material was so sheer that Yamashita could aim and shoot through it from up close. At the same time, anyone who might be inclined to fire back wouldn't be able to see him from more than a few yards away.

When the net was in place, Yamashita lay down just behind it on top of a cushion. His rifle barrel rested only a few millimeters from the netting. Cross sat a few feet away with a tablet computer on his lap. The tablet was synced to Brighton's UAV, providing a live feed from the drone's camera. After a quick comm-check and an all-ready report from Chief Walker, Cross set the operation in motion.

While they waited for the van and Shadid's limo to come into view, Yamashita said, "You've never taken overwatch before, Commander."

"True," Cross said. "But Chief Walker made the point last night that putting myself on the front lines every mission isn't exactly wise. So I'm trying this out." He hesitated then added, "Plus, I wasn't sure I could trust myself to behave if I had to ride in the limo with our VIP and Upton."

"Fair enough," Yamashita said.

Brighton was keeping the UAV high and centered, allowing Cross a good view of the route and the surrounding side streets. Four of Shadid's personal security guards rode in front of his limo on motorcycles, trying to ease the way through traffic. As they approached an intersection, two of the motorcycles pulled ahead and blocked the side streets so the limo's way would be clear. Then, while those two waited, the other pair of riders moved ahead to the next intersection. When intersections were close together, it made for a lot of stops and long pauses — and many unhappy morning commuters.

The small convoy came into view of the sniper's perch at last. At this point, they were half an hour behind schedule. "Got a visual," Yamashita murmured to Cross.

"So far so good," Cross said, his eyes glued to the tablet's screen. "You see anything?"

"It's clear," Yamashita said.

Below, the VIP's procession made a turn onto a side street with no cars on it. That street was the longest, straightest part of the route, offering overwatch the best field of view. The van and limo rolled down practically by themselves as the motorcycles leap-frogged ahead of them.

"Um, something's wrong here," Brighton's voice reported over the team's canalphones. "You see it too, Commander?"

"Yeah," Cross said with a tap on his earbud. "It's awfully quiet through this neighborhood. Where is everybody? I don't like this. Chief, tell your driver —"

A huge ball of dust and smoke blossomed on the street below, interrupting Cross. A second later came the boom and rattle of an explosion. A roadside bomb had detonated in a trash can at the intersection just behind the team's van. It did no damage to the vehicles, but the security man on the rear motorcycle disappeared in the fire and smoke. Another rider was knocked off his bike.

"IED!" Brighton shouted. "Where the —"

A second explosion went off across the street a little farther ahead, unseating the forward rider on that side.

"Chief, report!" Cross barked.

"We're secure!" Walker yelled over the earphones. The driver of Shadid's limo panicked and floored the accelerator. Wheels spun and smoked as the vehicle skidded away. "Hey, slow down, you maniac!"

"Stay on them!" Cross ordered.

"Sir," Paxton replied. He gunned the van's engine and took off after the fleeing limo.

"Yamashita, two blocks up," Cross said.

Two blocks ahead of the limo, a car came barreling down an alley on an intercept course. "Got it," Yamashita said. He took aim on the windshield for a closer look. "It's empty, sir."

Yamashita squeezed off a round into the car's engine block. A burst of flame and black smoke billowed from under the hood, but the shot came too late. Before the limo driver saw it, the burning car launched out of the alley and hit the limo in the

rear driver-side fender. The limo swerved, bounced onto the curb, and then rammed into the corner of a building.

Yamashita took a moment to scan up the alley where the car had come from. He saw a single figure at the far end — presumably the man who'd set the car in motion. He was running down the alley with a rifle in his hands. Yamashita pulled the trigger. The man collapsed.

"RPG!" Cross and Brighton called out at once.

"On top of the warehouse!" Cross added.

Yamashita swiveled his rifle toward the rooftop of the building across the street from where the limo had crashed. The first thing he saw was the open door on the roof-access stairway swinging closed. A second later, he saw a man in a black hood leaning over the edge of the roof with a rocket-propelled grenade launcher.

Yamashita and the masked man fired at the same time. The man on the roof toppled headlong off the warehouse, but not before his RPG streaked a line of white smoke through the air. The grenade hit the pavement just behind the limo's front-passenger tire. The car bucked and slammed down, thick smoke pouring out of its front end.

"Sergeant, get up here!" Walker yelled to Paxton over the earphone. When the chief transmitted, Yamashita could hear someone coughing. Then he heard Shadid's terrified grandson crying hysterically. It sent a primal shiver down Yamashita's spine to hear the boy howl. To force a child into this situation made the politician the lowest of the low.

"We're here," Paxton said. He whipped his van around the damaged limo. They stopped just ahead of the vehicle in the street.

"Chief, damage report," Cross said.

"Driver's dead," Walker responded. "Ursa Major has a broken leg; Ursa Minor is unhurt. Mister Know-It-All is unconscious."

"Hang tight," Cross said. He looked at Yamashita. "Do you see anybody else?"

With a long, steady sweep, Yamashita scanned the street for attackers. Then he traced a line up the side of a building overlooking the street from the opposite end of the neighborhood. "Streets are clear, sir," Yamashita said.

"Sir?" Walker called, his voice tense.

"All right, Chief," Cross replied. "Get the VIPs and Mister Know-It-All in the van. Ursa Minor first."

"Sir," Walker replied.

"I'll get the doors," Jannati said.

"I'm going to need some help with these other two," Williams said.

"I got it," Brighton replied.

Brighton hopped out of the passenger-side door of the van with his AA-12 combat shotgun. He ran back toward the limo as Jannati popped the van's back door open. Meanwhile, Chief Walker was half-climbing, half-falling out of the back passenger door of the limo with his M4 carbine in one hand and the wildly struggling Habib Shadid under his other arm.

"Whoa!" Cross shouted over the earphone. "Cover! TAKE COVER!"

Through his scope, Yamashita saw the metal door on the loading bay of a nearby warehouse roll upward to reveal a team of gunmen behind a makeshift barricade of oil drums and sandbags. The man in the middle of the team stood behind a tripod-mounted machine gun. As soon as the door cleared his firing line, the machine gunner took aim. Yamashita sighted on him at the same time. One shot to the chest put him down. As he fell, the gunner squeezed the trigger convulsively. Bullets sprayed out wildly. Careless impacts traced a line across the street between the limo and the van, just missing Brighton as he crossed through the gap. He dove back and shoulder-rolled to safety behind the van's open back door as Walker pulled Shadid's terrified grandson behind the open door of the limo.

In the warehouse, another of the gunmen pushed the dead man out of the way of the machine gun. Unfortunately, he stayed out of Yamashita's sights by ducking low, then sprayed bullets without looking. The shots chewed into the armor plating on the side of the van and broke up the pavement a bit, but did no serious damage. His fellows behind the barricade opened up with bullpup Khaybar rifles, pinning the Shadow Squadron soldiers inside or behind the vehicles.

"Covering fire!" Walker called out.

"Yamashita?" Cross asked.

"No shot, sir," the sniper said. He didn't have a clear line of sight to the gunmen to do more than waste a bullet on a minor wound. If the man spraying the MG3 would stop firing for just a second, Yamashita might be able to shoot it and take it out of commission. But that wasn't an option at the moment.

"All right," Cross said. He tapped his earphone. "Hot seat, you're up."

"Yes, sir!" Shepherd said, sounding a little too excited.

Brighton took a deep breath, then said, "I'm on it, sir," He hefted his AA-12 shotgun and whipped around the corner of the van hollering an inarticulate battle cry.

Yamashita saw a couple of the shooters pop up behind their Khaybars in surprise. He could have taken one or two of them down, but he knew Brighton had things under control. Brighton cleared his cover and opened fire with his combat shotgun on full auto. The weapon roared like a lion as he let fly. With a fire rate of 300 rounds per minute and a 12-gauge bore, the AA-12 filled the air with lead. One of the gunmen fell lifeless to the ground. Several shots punched into the barricade so hard that sand flew out like firework sparks.

Satisfied, Brighton dashed over to Walker's cover behind the limo's armored door and knelt down next to him. "Drum!" Brighton shouted, ejecting the shotgun's spent ammo drum.

Jannati threw him a second one from the back of the van. Brighton rammed it home and leaned around the edge of the limo. The bravest of the gunmen peeked out from cover to try his luck again.

Instead of aiming at the gunman, Brighton lined up his sight with the gun and let loose. The blasts knocked the weapon off its tripod.

"I'll take it from here," Shepherd said over the comm-channel.

Before the gunmen in the warehouse could peek out again, a circular hatch in the roof of the van popped open. Sergeant Shepherd rose through the opening behind a mounted M134 minigun. His back was to Yamashita, but the sniper was willing to bet that Shepherd was smiling from ear to ear.

"Light 'em up, Sergeant," Cross said, his voice cold and quiet.

"Hoorah!" Shepherd said.

Yamashita couldn't look away as Shepherd hit the firing button on the M134. Its six Gatling-style barrels spun up and put out a laser-accurate stream of 7.62x51mm NATO rounds at a rate just shy of 50 rounds per second. Whirring like a chainsaw, the minigun sprayed its ammo like a power hose spraying water. Shepherd swept an arc of fire across the kill zone, then back again. Bullets tore through the barricade like it was made of wet paper, annihilating the men behind it. None of them even had a chance to return fire before they were cut down.

A moment later, Shepherd let up to see if anyone returned fire or tried to run away. No one moved.

"Clear," Shepherd said, a smile evident in his voice.

"Roger that," Cross replied. "Chief, get the VIPs out of the limo and in the van before anybody else shows up."

"Sir," Walker said. Once more he began carrying Habib Shadid over toward the van. The boy had stopped struggling, but from the glimpse Yamashita caught of his face, it was because he was in shock.

When Walker was clear, Brighton ducked into the back of the limo. He emerged a moment later with Heshem Shadid. Williams was right behind the politician, gently pushing the older man along.

Yamashita began to scan the horizon, silently enjoying the look of pain he'd seen on Heshem Shadid's face. That's when Yamashita saw it: under cover of a rooftop ledge, a sniper was taking aim at something down below. Yamashita didn't have a clear shot from his position, but there was no mistaking the prone position and the gun barrel.

What happened next occurred in the span of a second, but to Yamashita's whirling thoughts it lasted much longer. Part of him wanted to watch and do nothing. He relished the thought of Heshem Shadid's final moments in this world filled with intense pain and fear. Yet as that savage thrill flickered inside him, disgust rose up and overwhelmed it. Was this who he was now, the sniper wondered? If Neil Larssen were still alive, would he be able to look his friend in the eye after what he was about to let happen? After this, would he be able to look at himself in the mirror? Would he ever see himself the same way, or would he always see his reflection glaring back with silent anger?

"No," Yamashita said. "No!" He tapped his earphone. "Brighton, get down! Sniper!"

Without a word, Brighton whipped the wobbling Shadid back around in a half circle and shoved him back toward Williams. At that precise instant, a bullet meant for Shadid's heart whizzed between his head and Brighton's.

The shot bounced off the armored roof of the limo. Williams pulled Shadid into the limo, then Brighton jumped in after him and slammed the door shut.

"Where is he?" Cross cried. He had Yamashita's rangefinder binoculars before his eyes, frantically scanning rooftops.

"He's in my sights," Yamashita said. He set his crosshairs on the muzzle flare as the sharpshooter — who could be none other than Zulfiqar himself — took his second shot. The projectile lodged in the bulletproof window.

"A little help here!" Brighton yelled.

Yamashita didn't give Zulfiqar another chance to fire. A quarter of a mile away, the silhouette of the enemy sniper jerked once, then slumped over sideways. The barrel of his rifle lifted up like a flag pole. For a moment, silence reigned, with nothing moving in that distant space.

Calm as ever came Yamashita's voice. "Clear."

* * *

Several hours later — once Shadid, his grandson, and Agent Upton were all safe in the van with the rest of Shadow

Squadron — Cross and Yamashita stood together over Zulfiqar's body. Two motorcycles they'd borrowed from Shadid's fallen bodyguards stood waiting for them downstairs.

Across the room, Zulfiqar's rifle — a variant of the Russian Dragunov sniper rifle — was still propped up where the man's fall had pinned it.

Cross pulled the rifle away from the dead man and ejected the ten-round box magazine onto the floor. "I told you we should've picked this place," he said, glancing out the window. "Best sniper perch in the neighborhood."

Yamashita leaned against the doorjamb to keep an eye out down the hallway. "I didn't want the best spot," the sniper said. "I wanted the second-best perch."

"Sure you did, Lieutenant," Cross said with a smirk. "Because you knew Zulfiqar would want the best sniper spot for himself? And you knew he'd just be waiting up there for his men to flush Shadid out of cover so he could take him out? Is that what you're trying to say?"

"I'm no mind reader, Commander," Yamashita said. "But this is the spot I would have chosen if I had wanted to kill Shadid."

"True," Cross said. "If you were Zulfiqar, you mean."

Cross left the man's body where it lay and faced Yamashita. The sniper met Cross's eyes warily.

"Then again," Cross said, "you're not Zulfiqar — you're you. If you had wanted Shadid dead, all you would've needed to do was hesitate at just the right moment . . . and watch as Zulfiqar took his shot."

Yamashita paused for a moment. Then he said, "If that's the kind of solider I was, then you'd have to keep me at arm's length during every mission. You'd have to be breathing down my neck at all times — looking over my shoulder to make sure I did the right thing."

"No," Cross said. His smirk and sarcastic tone were gone. In its place was an intensely serious, searching gaze that burned into Yamashita's eyes. "If you were that kind of soldier, you'd be off my team so fast it would make your head spin."

"Then I'm glad I'm not that type of soldier, Commander," Yamashita said.

As the words came out, Yamashita knew they were true. He'd flirted with temptation and had almost given in. But the regret he would have felt for the rest of his life stayed his hand.

Or rather, it had helped him pull the trigger.

"Good," Cross said, patting the sharpshooter on the back. "Let's keep it that way."

"Sir," Yamashita said, the hint of a smile on his face.

MISSION DEBRIEFING

OPERATION

SNIPER SHIELD 1234

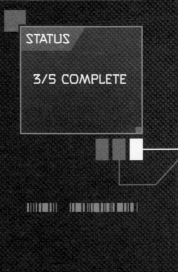

MISSION COMPLETE

PRIMARY OBJECTIVES

- Meet with the VIP and his personal security force

- Prep a route and determine an overwatch position for transit

- Protect the VIP en route to his destination

SECONDARY OBJECTIVES

x Avoid open conflict with Iraqi insurgents

x Keep our presence covert

STATUS

3/5 COMPLETE

3249.98

YAMASHITA, KIMIYO

RANK: Lieutenant
BRANCH: Army Ranger
PSYCH PROFILE: The team's sniper is an expert marksman and a true stoic. It seems his emotions are as steady as his trigger finger.

This operation was a perfect example of a worst-case scenario. Everything went wrong, the assigned tasks were complex and varied, and there was a fair amount of dislike for the VIP we were assigned to protect. But from the outside looking in, no one could have known it; our men performed with remarkable proficiency and courage, despite any reservations.

As for me, I can't say it was easy to safeguard the life of an evil man. But if I wanted *easy*, I wouldn't have chosen to become a sniper — or join Shadow Squadron.

— Lieutenant Kimiyo Yamashita

2019.691

AUTHOR DEBRIEFING

CARL BOWEN

Q/When and why did you decide to become a writer?

A/I've enjoyed writing ever since I was in elementary school. I wrote as much as I could, hoping to become the next Lloyd Alexander or Stephen King, but I didn't sell my first story until I was in college. It had been a long wait, but the day I saw my story in print was one of the best days of my life.

Q/What made you decide to write *Shadow Squadron*?

A/As a kid, my heroes were always brave knights or noble loners who fought because it was their duty, not for fame or glory. I think the special ops soldiers of the US military embody those ideals. Their jobs are difficult and often thankless, so I wanted to show how cool their jobs are, but also express my gratitude for our brave warriors.

Q/What inspires you to write?

A/My biggest inspiration is my family. My wife's love and support lifts me up when this job seems too hard to keep going. My son is another big inspiration.

He's three years old, and I want him to read my books and feel the same way I did when I read my favorite books as a kid. And if he happens to grow up to become an elite soldier in the US military, that would be pretty awesome, too.

Q/Describe what it was like to write these books.
A/The only military experience I have is a year I spent in the Army ROTC. It gave me a great respect for the military and its soldiers, but I quickly realized I would have made a pretty awful soldier. I recently got to test out a friend's arsenal of firearms, including a combat shotgun, an AR-15 rifle, and a Barrett M82 sniper rifle. We got to blow apart an old fax machine.

Q/What is your favorite book, movie, and game?
A/My favorite book of all time is *Don Quixote*. It's crazy and it makes me laugh. My favorite movie is either *Casablanca* or *Double Indemnity*, old black-and-white movies made before I was born. My favorite game, hands down, is *Skyrim*, in which you play a heroic dragonslayer. But not even *Skyrim* can keep me from writing more *Shadow Squadron* stories, so you won't have to wait long to read more about Ryan Cross and his team. That's a promise.

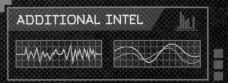
ARTIST

WILSON TORTOSA

Wilson "Wunan" Tortosa is a Filipino comic book artist best known for his works on *Tomb Raider* and the American relaunch of *Battle of the Planets* for Top Cow Productions. Wilson attended Philippine Cultural High School, then went on to the University of Santo Tomas, where he graduated with a Bachelor's Degree in Fine Arts, majoring in Advertising.

COLORIST

BENNY FUENTES

Benny Fuentes lives in Villahermosa, Tabasco, in Mexico, where the temperature is just as hot as the sauce. He studied graphic design in college, but now he works as a full-time colorist in the comic book and graphic novel industry for companies like Marvel, DC Comics, and Top Cow Productions. He shares his home with two crazy cats, Chelo and Kitty, who act like they own the place.

3245.98

31901055181483

SIGNING OFF